TARTAN MAGIC

The Wizard's Map

Jane Yolen

HARCOURT BRACE & COMPANY

San Diego   New York   London

Library of Congress Cataloguing-in-Publication Data
Yolen, Jane.
The wizard's map/Jane Yolen.
p.   cm.
"Tartan magic, book one."
Summary: Three children visiting relatives in Scotland
become involved in the plans of a diabolical wizard.
ISBN 0-15-202067-5
[1. Magic—Fiction. 2. Wizards—Fiction.
3. Scotland—Fiction. 4. Twins—Fiction.]
I. Title.
PZ7.Y78Wm   1999
[Fic]—dc21   98-33889

Text set in Galliard Old Style
Display type set in Goudy Medieval
Designed by Judythe Sieck

Printed in the United States of America
D F H J L M K I G E

For Jenny and Gordon McIlreavy
and their parents,
part of our Scottish sojourn

Contents

Tartan:
Plaid cloth.
In Scotland each clan
has its own distinctive pattern.

The
Wizard's
Map

One

Impatience

Are we almost there?" Jennifer asked for what must have been the hundredth time.

"Honestly," Mom said, "the one thing you kids don't seem to have is any patience. We'll be there soon enough."

They went around a deep bend in the rain-slick road and only Molly, asleep in her car seat, seemed oblivious to the swervings of the car.

Then Peter asked the same question, only he said it slightly differently. "Are we there yet?"

"I hate to repeat myself—" Mom began, but Pop interrupted her by pointing out the befogged car window at a sign that read FAIRBURN. It was a dangerous thing to do, since he was driving on the left side of the road for the first time. "There it is—Fairburn."

The car swerved perilously again.

Jennifer looked out of the window to where stone walls seemed to anchor the fields. The few trees stood like green sentinels before a grey outcropping of rock. All were drenched with the rain.

"That hill?" asked Peter. "That's Fairburn?" His voice held as much scorn as a thirteen-year-old could muster. He hadn't come happily across the Atlantic to Scotland for the summer, leaving his friends and teammates behind.

"Don't be silly," Jennifer said. As Peter's twin, she was allowed to say such things but rarely did. He was the more aggressive of the two, having entered the world with an angry yell, while she— or so her mother always said—had slid out quietly, smiling. "That's where it all begins."

By "all," Jennifer merely meant the little town at the foot of the Highlands, and their summer away from Connecticut. What she didn't know was that this was also the beginning of an adventure that would take them through the dark turnings of a wizard's cave and into Time itself.

"Tidy yourselves," Mom said, moving comfortably back into the rhythms and slang of her Scottish childhood. "I want Gran and Da to have a fine first impression of you."

Gran and Da weren't Mom's real grandparents. They were actually some older cousins who had helped raise her after her own parents had died in a car crash. In fact they were the *only* family Mom still had. She phoned them once a month, but had only been back to visit a couple of times since moving to America to go to college. And that, Jennifer knew, had happened an awfully long time ago.

Jennifer never really listened closely to her mother's stories about the dead Douglas side of the family, preferring to hear about the living. Therefore she knew much more about her father's relatives, especially Granny and Granfa Dyer, who lived only three states away and had built Peter and Jennifer and Molly a medieval castle out of wood painted to look like stone, big enough for three children to stand up in and gaze out over the towers.

Only four-year-old Molly still played in the castle, of course, moving her dolls in and out for regular royal tea parties and wearing one of Granfa Dyer's cardboard crowns atop her dark curls. Jennifer sometimes wished that she could still participate in their old make-believe games; only, she knew that if she did, Peter would laugh at her. Peter and all his friends. Since she desperately wanted them to think well of her, she'd left the castle and her dolls behind.

As the car shot by the hill—which was marked with a sign warning about slippery conditions in the rain—Pop floored the gas pedal. That sent the car careening around a curve, and for several perilous seconds it hugged the right side of the road. Then when the road suddenly straightened, Pop appeared to remember they were in Scotland and he pulled the wheel abruptly to the left.

Jennifer let out a little shriek and Mom moaned, but Peter merely shrank down inside himself further than he'd been before, as if he were more embarrassed than scared. They were all so busy reacting to the car's erratic movement that they were startled when the actual town of Fairburn rose up ahead of them, a grey presence in the slackening rain. It seemed surrounded by a stone wall and looked like a medieval fortress in a movie.

"*Braveheart*," Jennifer said.

"*Rob Roy*," Peter corrected. He was closer to the right century. Except most of Fairburn's wall had tumbled down ages earlier, and only the West Gate and a few sections still remained.

Half a dozen Japanese tourists, dressed in water-proof coats and hats, were standing on the fallen-down part of the wall, busily snapping photos of one another. Two young men in colorful kilts and short dark jackets, their knees well burnished by the cold rain, strolled by.

"Bet that will keep out any enemies," Peter said sarcastically.

"What will?" asked Jennifer.

"That wall," Peter explained.

"What enemies?" Jennifer persisted.

Peter was about to answer her back with some sharp, quick, petulant response, when Molly—who'd been drowsing since they left Edinburgh Airport—woke up in the car seat with a start.

"Rainbow!" she cried.

And there, over all of Fairburn, was a sudden fantastic rainbow enclosing the town as gracefully above as the wall did below. The rainstorm, it seemed, was over.

"Welcome home," Pop said, talking to the entire family.

Molly was the only one who smiled.

TWO

Welcome

They turned down a street with the strange name of Burial Brae, and then right onto another much narrower road with as odd a name—Double Dykes. The car bumped unrelentingly over the cobblestones until Jennifer thought her teeth would fall out from the pounding. At last Mom gave a little screech.

"There!" she cried. "There!"

"There" was a lane marked ABBOT'S CLOSE. Jennifer recognized it at once, having written the address down for all her friends a dozen times: Scot's Cottage, 13 Abbot's Close, Fairburn, Fife, Scotland. Mom had explained that Fife was like a state but was called a kingdom so Jennifer had told all her friends that she was spending the summer in a cottage in a Scottish kingdom, and they'd all been suitably impressed.

But when the car pulled up to number 13, it was not anything like a cottage at all. Rather it was an enormous, whitewashed, two-story building with a small window in the attic and a grey slate roof that slumped like a farmer's hat.

"I thought a cottage was something small and cozy..." Jennifer began.

"Or with two rooms and a big fireplace," added Peter. It often happened that they had similar ideas about things.

But Molly said what they had all been thinking ever since spotting the house. "Magic!" she breathed.

Just as Molly spoke, the door opened and two people walked out, their arms opened wide in welcome.

Mom screeched again. "It's Gran and Da!"

"Well, who else would it be," Peter mumbled, and Jennifer elbowed him hard. He was so surprised—for Jennifer was usually the compliant one—that he didn't protest, but shut up at once.

Gran and Da had round faces, browned and seamed from the sun, topped with hair as flat white as the walls of their cottage. Gran was wearing a long greenish tartan skirt and a sweater set,

Da heavy brown trousers, a plaid shirt, and a tweed jacket.

"They look like Niddy and Noddy," Molly said. She meant they looked like her Scottish dolls, the ones that went in and out of Granfa Dyer's castle a dozen times a day. And except for the color of their hair, she was right.

"That's the Douglas plaid," said Jennifer, remembering the gifts that Gran had sent ahead to them.

"Well, don't expect me to wear it," Peter remarked sullenly, to the entire car.

But Mom ignored them all, throwing open her door and running into Gran's and Da's arms as a child would. They did not seem startled by her buoyant enthusiasm, but covered her face with kisses.

"I thought," Pop said slowly, "that the Scots were supposed to be a reserved people."

Suddenly, as if remembering that she was a grown-up, Mom led Gran and Da over to the car. Opening the back door, she got Molly out of the car seat and held her up to Da, who took her in his arms. "Look at those curls, that heart-shaped face. Why—she's the spit of your mum."

"And this," Mom said, pulling Peter out of the car, "is Peter."

Peter grunted and put out his hand to forestall any kisses. Da shook it with his free hand, but Gran ignored Peter's hand and smothered him in her arms.

Jennifer got out of the car herself and stood quietly, smoothing down her sweater. "I'm Jennifer," she said.

"My wee namesake," said Gran.

"She looks like you did at her age," said Da to Gran. "The straight red hair falling over her eyes. There's magic in those green eyes. Magic."

Jennifer suddenly felt terribly uncomfortable. It was one thing for someone Molly's age to speak of magic. She was just four years old, after all. That sort of thing was expected. But for a grown-up to talk about magic so matter-of-factly was plain embarrassing.

"Color magic, at the very least," Gran agreed. "And maybe more."

Jennifer looked over at Peter, hoping to catch his eye. But he was too busy stalking down the road, trying to get his equilibrium back, to notice. He hated being hugged, especially by strangers, and it might take him a five full minutes of walk-about, which is what Pop called it, before he was sociable again. So Jennifer did the only thing she could do in the circumstances—she looked down at the cobblestones and blushed.

"And she takes a compliment like you do, too," Da said. "That's a braw blush, like a rose."

They laughed, and Mom and Pop unaccountably laughed with them. Jennifer thought with sudden misery that grown-ups could always be counted on to make a joke at a kid's expense, and she turned on her heel, following Peter down the road. The grown-ups' laughter, like a shadow, trailed behind.

When she was too far away to be heard by the others, Jennifer called out in a strained voice, "Peter! Peter! Wait!"

He didn't stop, but he did slow down so that she could catch up. She noticed that his normally ruddy face was blanched. He looked the way he did when he was coming down with a fever: drawn and white.

For a while they walked side by side in silence along the cobbled lane. Not even the wind troubled the trees. Jennifer thought suddenly, *This sure isn't Connecticut.* She didn't know anyplace in America quite this quiet. Straining to hear some ordinary sound, she finally smiled when at last she heard the far-off yapping of a dog.

"Peter," she said again, this time in her normal voice.

He turned and looked at her, and his face seemed suddenly older, unfamiliar, dark with unexpressed emotion. Jennifer shuddered without meaning to. Then, as if a wing, or the shadow of a wing, had passed across him, his face lightened, color flooded back into it, and he drew his right hand through his lank brown hair.

"I bet we're all just tired," he said. "I mean, all that time in a plane. I sure didn't get any sleep." He was never one for a real apology.

"You slept like a log," Jennifer said. "Snoring, too. I heard you."

"Heard me?" Peter laughed his old Peter laugh, and Jennifer was relieved to hear it. "How could you? You were fast asleep yourself."

"I didn't sleep at all," Jennifer argued.

"Not even a bit?"

"Well, a *wee* bit," Jennifer said, using one of the

few Scottish words she knew and had practiced.

And they turned together without comment—the "twin thing," their father always called it—going back to the cottage and whatever waited for them there.

Three

Gran's Garden

Exhausted from the long trip, they all napped and then woke to late-afternoon sunshine. After a hearty dinner, which Gran called "tea," and a cream cake for dessert, which Da unaccountably called "pudding," they got to wander around the walled garden behind the cottage.

"You'll not see the likes of that garden elsewhere," Da said, to Gran's blush. "Herbal magic is Gran's specialty. Folks come from miles around to view it."

"Not miles, now. Just neighbors."

"*Must* be miles, then," muttered Peter. "There aren't any neighbors." No one but Jennifer heard him.

"Tomorrow," Mom promised, "we'll show you the town. It's got a castle."

Molly clapped. "A real castle!"

Laughing, Pop ruffled her curls. "I thought you had a real castle at home, squirt."

Molly looked up at him with disdain. "That's just painted wood," she said.

"Which doesn't make it any less real," Pop replied.

But Molly gave him another look, which combined disdain with a kind of pint-sized ferocity, and he dropped the subject.

"Why not now?" Peter asked.

"Everything's closed down. It's night," Gran said.

Jennifer looked out the window, where, even though it was nine o'clock, the sun was still high overhead. Summer in Scotland had what Mom had called "white nights."

Night! It was bright as day.

■ ■ ■

The garden was larger than their entire Connecticut front and back yards combined. It came in two parts. Next to the house there was a formal garden, the borders planted with purple-clustered flowers interspersed with pansies, whose little monkey-faced flowers nodded in the breeze. Low mounds of heather, spidery bursts of anemones, a riot of lavender, and grave thrusts of iris and loosestrife crowded together in one colorful plot. Old rosebushes filled another, their spindly arms still supporting a profusion of blooms.

There was a knot of herbs in a small raised area by the kitchen door. Jennifer could identify mint and parsley, which grew in their garden at home. Gran was just pointing out some more—"Chervil, rosemary, sage, and catnip"—when Mom steered Gran away.

"How strange," Jennifer said to herself. "Catnip in with the herbs!" But then the rest of the garden was so wonderful, she gave it no more thought.

Scattered along the paved stone path were old stone troughs filled with blue and purple lobelia trailing bright flowers over the sides. An armless cherub stood sentinel at one of the branchings of the path, at its feet a pot of multicolored petunias.

"Come see!" Jennifer called to Peter, but he was much too busy trying to send a wooden croquet ball through a series of wire wickets on the strangely flattened lawn, hitting the ball with quick, angry slaps of the mallet.

"Trust Peter," Jennifer muttered to herself, "to find a game."

She looked to see what the rest of the family

was doing. Pop was discussing something earnestly with Da, pointing to the cottage roof, his hands making conversation as well. Mom and Gran were sitting together on a wicker settee, with Molly between them. Molly was asleep again, and the two adults chatted companionably over her. Mom's right hand rested on Molly's back, rising and falling with Molly's every breath.

Since no one was paying the slightest attention to her, Jennifer headed down toward the back garden by herself, the one Gran had called "the old garden."

The stone walkway to the old garden wound through the rose arbor and around a great holm oak whose massive trunk was bound around by an ironwork seat. Jennifer paused to look at the seat because the three wrought-iron legs had been twisted and shaped into fanciful designs. One leg looked like a slender coursing dog, another like an elongated dragon with its wings swept back against its sides, the third like an attenuated unicorn standing on its rear legs with its horn poking up into the seat. Jennifer ran her fingers over the designs. The metal was strangely cold to the touch and made her tremble.

"What a ninny I am," she said aloud. She liked the word. It came from her reading. No one in school used it. "Ninny!" she said again. Then she headed on down the path, which turned abruptly into a gravel road.

On her left was a high stone wall covered with vines. A few hardy flowers clung to the crevices, and moss had invaded the chinks. The wall effectively hid Gran and Da's cottage from view.

On her right was a veritable forest, though how a forest could be in somebody's backyard, Jennifer could not imagine. The woods looked ancient, with enormous dark, brooding trees and a thick, wiry underbrush. Someone had obviously trimmed back what limbs hung over the path and what brush crept forward toward the gravel, but Jennifer could imagine it was a battle waged every year.

She heard something scrabbling in the undergrowth and stopped for a moment, frightened. Her heart pounded in her chest, in her ears. Then she reminded herself that there were few big animals in Scotland, and only one snake—the adder—which was rare, and rarely seen. Mom had made Jennifer and Peter read up on Scotland before the trip. And after all, this was a *walled* garden. Nothing large or threatening could possibly get in.

A little white cat, hardly more than a kitten, shot out onto the gravel path from the woods, took one look at Jennifer, and raced back the way it had come.

Jennifer laughed out loud at having been so frightened by something so small, and plunged in between the trees after the cat.

The minute she was under the trees, what had been a sunny evening became dark. Only every now and then a shaft of filtered light rayed down from above, as if illuminating another kind of path scratched out on the forest floor.

Jennifer knew she could not possibly get very lost. The trees were a part of Gran's walled garden, not a trackless woods. So she didn't take particular care to watch where she was going. She just blundered along, pushing aside any interlacings of vines that got in her way.

After about ten minutes of hard slogging, and quite a few scratches from hidden thorns, she was rewarded by stumbling into a little glade that was in full sunshine. In the center of the glade was a lovely little one-room white house made of wicker and wood. The white cat was curled in a corner of the front step, fast asleep.

"So there you are," said Jennifer.

At her voice the cat woke in fright, leaped to its feet, and disappeared around the side of the house.

Jennifer had walked all around the little cottage and was about to try the front door when she heard her name being called. She thought it was Gran's voice, but it was so filtered through the surrounding trees, she couldn't be sure.

"I'm here!" she called back. "At the little garden house."

It suddenly started to rain again, not the quiet, cozy rain of Connecticut, but a terrible, bucketing downpour. She rattled the cottage's door handle, thinking she could wait out the rain in there, but the door was locked.

"Bother!" she told herself, one of her mother's favorite expressions, then she plunged back into the tangled woods. At least there she could take shelter from the rain.

But when it began to thunder ominously, fear of lightning drove her deeper and deeper into the woods until, with a crash, she found herself tumbling out onto the gravel path right at Gran's feet.

The gravel path was dry.

"Never," Gran said, "go into that wood without protection."

"I don't have my raincoat unpacked yet," Jennifer said.

"We've got plenty of protection to go around," said Gran. "You just need to ask." And, with her hand expertly cupping Jennifer's elbow, Gran led her quickly back to the house.

FOUR

Attic Games

The next day it rained again—a hard, steady rain with gale-force winds. The television news predicted a full day of the same.

"It will be nice enough tomorrow," promised Gran. "Scotland is like that. After every shower, a rainbow."

"And after every rainbow, a shower," muttered Peter.

"You can play in the attic," added Da. "Plenty of stuff up there to do."

Molly was immediately excited, but Jennifer and Peter exchanged glances.

"Old clothes," said Gran. "For dress-up."

"We," Peter said slowly, "are too old for dress-up."

Jennifer tried to soften what he'd just said so he didn't sound like a complete toad. "Peter's never been interested in that sort of thing."

"And old games," added Da. "Maps. Books. Photographs."

Peter was unmoved.

"And a hidden room," Da finished.

"Da..." Mom sounded a warning note.

It was too late. Peter had looked up at the last and was staring avidly at Da.

"A hidden room!" There was a great deal of awe in his voice.

"Which we know about but have never found," added Gran.

"But you've lived here forever," Jennifer said.

"We've lived here for a long time," agreed Gran. "And my parents before that. But the house has been here even longer."

"How long?" asked Molly.

"*This* house, since the fifteenth century."

"Is that long?" Molly asked.

"Hundreds and hundreds of years," Jennifer said, wondering exactly what Gran had meant by "*this* house."

"Five hundred years," said Peter precisely.

"Gosh!" said Molly. "That's older than Granfa Dyer."

They all laughed, and whatever tension had

been brought into the room by the grey rain disappeared.

"Who wants to see that attic now?" asked Gran.

All three of them shot their hands into the air, and the day was decided.

■ ■ ■

The attic was on the third floor, though Gran and Da called it the second floor, the first floor being known as the ground floor.

"I thought," Peter whispered to Jennifer, "that we all spoke the same language. But we don't."

"It's all English," explained Jennifer. "Just not *American* English."

"Here we are." Gran opened a hallway door, revealing a set of stone steps that curved up into the darkness.

"Are you coming?" Molly asked Gran.

"There's no need," said Gran. "At least not now." She hesitated. "Take the torch." Then she handed Peter a flashlight.

"See," Peter said to Jennifer. "Not what I mean by 'torch.' "

"You'll find a switch near the top of the stairs. On the left. And, Jennifer—you take this dust cloth." She handed a Douglas plaid tea towel to Jennifer and, so saying, left them to their own devices. They could hear her footsteps clattering down to the floor below, and then farther down, till they could hear nothing at all.

Peter went first with the torch, and when he got to the top of the stairs called down. "I found it. Only it's on the right, not the left. Hold on." A second later an overhead light flooded down, illuminating the well-worn steps.

Holding Molly's hand, Jennifer went up the stairs. At the top, she stopped and looked around. Even with the light, the attic was filled with shadows. Or maybe because of it. Jennifer was not sure.

"Look at all the dust," said Molly. She wrote her name in big clumsy letters on the top of a trunk. Her name was the only thing she knew how to write, though she could already read.

Using the tea towel, Jennifer wiped off the top of the trunk, erasing Molly's name as she did so. Then she lifted up the lid.

"Look!" cried Molly. "Dress-up." She pulled out a white frilly apron and a very small and delicately laced white dress.

"That's for a christening," explained Jennifer. "You wore one of those when you were a baby."

"Where is it?" asked Molly. "I've never seen it."

"Maybe..." Jennifer said in a spooky voice, "maybe this is the very one." She pounced on Molly and began tickling her until Molly's giggles threatened to turn into sobs.

They unpacked the rest of the trunk together, finding a dress covered all over with black beads, a long crimson cloak lined with some kind of fur, a plain light brown turban, a soldier's uniform jacket with gold braid on the shoulders and three medals with bright ribbons pinned to the chest, and a silver crest that said A DOUGLAS.

"Peter, look at this," Jennifer said, standing and holding the turban. She brought it over to Peter, who was busy tapping on a wall. "What are you doing?"

"Trying to find the secret room, of course," Peter said. "But nothing sounds hollow.... Wait a minute. Do you think this one sounds right?" The wall he was rapping on had a window high up under the eaves.

"Don't be stupid," said Jennifer. "That's an outside wall."

Peter looked up and realized how foolish he'd been. "Oh—right."

"I'll help, though," Jennifer said, laying the turban aside. They went slowly around the room three times, knocking solemnly, until Mom came to the foot of the stairs and called them all down for lunch.

■ ■ ■

It was still dreary outside, the rain coming down in sheets. Gran called it "dreech."

"I like that word," said Molly. "*Dreech.* It sounds like what it is."

"Onomatopoeia," said Jennifer, and Peter nodded. "We learned about that in school." Even as she said it, she was thinking that school, with its concrete walls and concrete playground, seemed very far away.

"We haven't found the hidden room yet," Peter told Gran. "Can you give us a hint?"

"I told you we've never found it," Gran replied, setting another kind of cake in front of him.

"I thought that was—you know—a kind of come-on," Peter said.

"Come-on?" Gran looked confused and turned to Mom.

"A tease, Gran. A riddle," Mom said.

"Oh, aye," Gran said. "It's a riddle, all right. Only, we've never managed to solve it. Perhaps it's waiting for the right bairn to come along."

"*Bairn?*" Molly asked.

"Child," said Jennifer. It was the second Scottish word she'd memorized. "It means child."

■ ■ ■

They finished their pudding and raced up the stairs, Peter going ahead and taking the steps two at a time. Back in the attic, Molly headed toward another trunk that was sitting against a far wall, but Peter and Jennifer made the rounds again, tapping and listening, and tapping again.

They stopped for a while to figure out a series of games played with two packs of cards that Molly had found in the trunk. The cards were kept in a small blue box with the word *Patience* in gold script on the top.

"Mom always says we need to learn patience," Peter said. "So here goes!"

Jennifer giggled, and on hearing her sister laugh, Molly wanted to know the joke. Even when it was explained, she didn't understand, but she laughed anyway, not wanting to be left out.

A booklet detailing the rules came with the cards. According to the booklet's first page, it had been published in 1933.

"That's even before Mom and Pop were born," said Jennifer.

"Even before Granny and Granfa Dyer," added Peter.

"Are you sure?" Jennifer asked.

He nodded.

"Wow," said Molly.

Jennifer scanned the contents page over Peter's shoulder. The games had names like The Sultan and Puss in the Corner and The Demon.

"The Demon!" Peter said. "Let's try that one." He read out the instructions. They were much too difficult for Molly, and she soon lost interest, drifting back to the costumes. In a third trunk she found a china-head doll, which she dressed in the christening gown.

"No patience at all!" Jennifer and Peter said together, then laughed. They took turns reading the rest of the instructions aloud. The cards were to be set out in individual patterns called "tableaux," and each game had a different setting. Any cards remaining in the hand were called "talon," and the discarded cards that did not fit into the patterns properly were called "the rubbish heap." Cards not used in a particular game were known as "dead."

"Pretty gruesome," Peter said happily, though even he found The Demon instructions too difficult to understand. "Better start with the first game and work our way through." He laid out the cards for The Star.

Though the games were all forms of solitaire, the twins worked on the first together. It was too easy, and they finished it in minutes, so they progressed to the next one in the booklet, the one called The Sultan. Peter put the tan turban on his head, rolled his eyes dramatically, and set the cards down with a flourish.

Jennifer laughed, watching Peter's progress for a while. Then she looked over her shoulder to check up on Molly.

Molly was hunched over a small table, making designs with a pen on a piece of paper.

"What are you writing on, Molls?" Jennifer asked.

"Just an old piece of paper," Molly said. "I found it in the doll's pocket."

"Oh-oh," Peter said, jumping up. The turban fell off his head.

Jennifer beat him to Molly's side and snatched at the paper.

"Mine!" Molly said, and Jennifer knew she'd have to cozen her sister or else the paper would be torn in two.

"Can I see what you've done, Molls?" Jennifer asked. "Can I see your drawing? I think you're the best drawer in the family." It wasn't a lie at all. Jennifer and Peter had not an ounce of art between them.

"OK," Molly said, reluctantly handing over the paper.

"Oh, Molls, what have you done!" Jennifer held it up to the light.

The paper was an old beige map. It was torn along the edges. What Molly had done was to draw a sequence of seven awkward circles in a row across the bottom of the map. There was a long line coming from the last circle, where her pen had slipped when Jennifer tried to snatch the paper away.

"Maps are valuable, Molls," Peter said. "Especially old maps like this. You can't just draw on them."

"But I *want* to draw," Molly wailed.

Jennifer and Peter looked at one another, and Jennifer said, "Mom's got your coloring books downstairs. And you know what?"

"What?" asked Molly, distracted for the moment.

"It's time for tea!" said Peter.

"More pudding?"

"Always," Jennifer and Peter said together.

Molly turned and raced down the steps, not even bothering to hold on to the wooden banister—a maneuver as fraught with danger as Pop's driving on the left in the rain.

Quietly tucking the map in her sweater pocket, Jennifer followed behind Molly, ready to help if she slipped.

Peter was last down the stairs, carefully turning off the light as he went. The cards were still spread out in The Sultan pattern, the turban tumbled next to them. Peter had been ahead in the game; he didn't want to put the cards away.

FIVE

The Map

While Molly and Peter gobbled up the pudding—it was carrot cake this time, drenched in cream—Jennifer took Gran aside into the pantry.

"The attic is great," Jennifer said. "Lots of surprises."

"Maybe more than you know," said Gran. "But not more than you can handle."

Jennifer thought this was a very odd thing to say, but she was beginning to think that Gran was a bit odd herself. Still, Jennifer had brought the map down to show Gran, because she suspected it might be valuable. Drawing the map out of her pocket, she said, "We found this in one of the trunks. Or rather, Molly found it. But she didn't know any better—and she scribbled on it." Then she added quickly, "Molly's only four, after all." As she spoke she unfolded the map and handed it to Gran. It made a strange noise, like faraway firecrackers. "I don't think she's ruined it, though. We stopped her in—"

Gran's face paled. She reached out with a trembling hand for the map. "Michael Scot's map!" she said. "O Scotland, that he once drew ye. I thought the blasted thing gone for good." Then she stared at the map, put her other hand to her forehead, and looked as if she were about to pass out.

"Da! Da!" Jennifer cried frantically. "Come quick!" She put her arms around the old woman and helped her to a ladder-back chair at the kitchen table.

Molly saw the beige paper map in Gran's hand and burst into tears. "I didn't mean it," she cried, her mouth full of cake. "I didn't mean it!"

Da raced in from the living room with Mom and Pop at his heels. It took some time before the sobbing child and the fainting woman were comforted, and only after everyone was completely calm could the story of the map be told.

But at last Molly was "molly-fied," as Pop said, with an extra helping of pudding all around. And Gran had caught her breath, the rose color creeping slowly back into her cheeks.

"What about the map?" Jennifer ventured when

all was quiet again. "And who is Michael Scot?"

"An evil man," said Da. "With a de'il of a horse." He saw they didn't understand him and he added, "De'il, you know. A devil!" He said it with the kind of vehemence reserved for personal enemies. It was the way Pop spoke about their state senator.

"Michael Scot is an astrologer," said Gran. "And court physician to the emperor."

"Wait a minute," said Peter, putting down his fork. "What emperor? There aren't any emperors around now."

"There were in the thirteenth century," said Gran. "Which is when Michael Scot first lived."

Pop shook his head. "What's a thirteenth-century map doing stuffed in a trunk in your attic? Surely it should be in a museum."

"It didn't look like any thirteenth-century map to me," said Peter.

"What do *you* know of the thirteenth century?" said Jennifer, too fascinated by what was happening to realize that she had just challenged Peter in public.

"Well, I know they didn't write like *that* in the thirteenth century. Don't you remember, Jen, when we studied printing in fifth grade? That was fifteenth century—Gutenberg and all that stuff. You can hardly read anything written back then. And look!" He nodded his head toward the map, which was the color of a grocery bag, and crinkled with wear.

They all looked. And Molly, with the slow articulation of a new reader, read aloud what was written at the top of the page:

MICHAEL...SCOT...HIS...OWN...MAP

She stumbled a bit on the first word.

"That's almost modern writing!" said Peter triumphantly.

"Michael Scot is a wizard," said Gran. "He can move through time. The map is only as old as the last time he was in this house, a hundred years ago. It mirrors his heart. Once this was the map of all Scotland, and Michael Scot had the country in his hand. Then it was the map of the kingdom of Fife. And now it is but a map of Fairburn, so small has he grown in his confinement."

"This is a story—right?" Jennifer said.

But Gran shook her head. "Not exactly, child. This is magic."

"Michael Scot's magic," added Da.

"But magic is—" Jennifer began. She was going to say "book stuff." But Gran interrupted.

"You Americans need to understand this about magic. There are seven kinds: Major Arcana and Minor." Her face was deadly serious.

Peter rolled his eyes and left the room.

Gran paid him no mind, but continued. "The Major consist of earth magic, air magic, fire magic, and water magic. The Minor magics are colors, numbers, and riddles. White magic is the proper use of the gift, and black magic is done by the wicked. Tartan magic is . . ."

Reluctantly, Jennifer followed Peter out of the room.

In the hall, Peter turned on her. "The syrup has definitely slipped off Gran's pancake," he said. "She's half a sandwich shy of a picnic." He and his friends collected such sayings. "The bell's ringing but no one's home." He grimaced. "And so are the rest of you, if you listen to her. She's one batty old lady."

"She's our *Gran*," Jennifer said, touching his arm as if to emphasize what she was saying.

"She's not our Gran!" he reminded her. "She's

just a dotty old Scottish cousin of Mom's who took care of Mom aeons ago. Probably has Alzheimer's."

"Peter, how can you say that?" Jennifer stared at Peter. *He's changed,* she thought. *He never used to be so mean-mouthed.*

"Grow up, Jen, and think. One minute Gran says this Michael Scot character lived in the thirteenth century, and the next she says he was in this house a hundred years ago. And then she says he drew a map of Scotland, but now it's a map of Fairburn. Didn't you see it has street names? And then she says the map is as old as the last time he was in the house. Right! And then all this stuff about earth magic and color magic and arcanas. She should be put in the loony bin."

Jennifer couldn't think of a single reason to disagree.

Peter started toward the stairs. "I'm going up to finish that Patience game." Speaking over his shoulder, he added, *"Alone."*

She didn't follow him. When Peter said he wanted to be alone, he always meant it. Instead she went back into the kitchen, where the grown-ups and Molly were huddled over the map.

"The circles are down here," Gran was saying, pointing to the bottom edge of the map. "South of Fairburn."

"That's McIlreavy's farm," said Da. "He's planted it in corn."

"I love corn," said Molly.

"Da means wheat. For bread," explained Mom.

"He said *corn*." Molly was adamant. "Corn's not wheat."

" 'Corn' doesn't mean corn here in Scotland," said Mom. "It means—"

But before she could repeat herself, Peter stormed into the room, his voice graveled with anger. "All right—who did it? Who finished The Sultan?"

For someone had completed the Patience game and then, ever so carefully, had put the turban on top of the trunk.

SIX

Secrets

No one would own up to having finished Peter's game, and he was furious.

"We were all down here together," Jennifer told him sensibly.

"Not everyone," said Peter. He meant that Mom and Pop and Da had been in the living room while the children were having their tea with Gran in the kitchen. In the living room and out of sight.

But it was unthinkable that any of *them* would have sneaked up the back stairs to the attic in order to finish a game they hadn't even known Peter was playing. There was no reason for them to go up in the attic to play such a trick. And besides, Mom and Pop didn't know how to play Patience.

"Or so they say," Peter grumbled to Jennifer, but out of the grown-ups' hearing.

"Should we go up again?" Jennifer ventured. "Just to check things out?" She wasn't keen to do it, but thought she should make the offer.

Peter was strangely reluctant as well.

Molly was the only one of the three who wanted to head back to the attic, because she wanted to bring down the doll in the christening gown. However, she didn't want to go up alone. "Because of the shadders," she said.

And thinking about the shadows, Jennifer felt suddenly cold.

"No," Jennifer told her. "We won't go."

"No," Peter confirmed.

And when Molly went whining to Gran, Gran was firm about her staying downstairs as well. "Not enough light. Tomorrow is soon enough." And since it was Gran's house, Molly had to be content with that.

The twins looked at one another, nodding, relief clearly written on both their faces, though they hadn't said anything out loud.

■ ■ ■

Later that evening Peter brought the mystery up again, as they were brushing their teeth.

"Do you think Da did it?" he asked. He was reluctant to let the thing go.

"Did what?" Jennifer asked, though she knew what he meant.

"Did Da finish the Patience game? And if so, why?"

Jennifer was almost sure that before coming downstairs Peter had finished the game himself and had forgotten. Or at least she had convinced herself of that. Any other explanation was too scary to contemplate. Especially remembering the look that had been exchanged by Gran and Da over Peter's head when he'd come stumbling into the kitchen.

She knew it had to be that Peter had forgotten, because he was not a practical joker. In fact, he hated being teased and, consequently, never teased anyone else.

Still, Jennifer thought suddenly, Peter had already seemed different in Scotland. Maybe there would be more changes.

"I don't think so," she said in a voice that was hesitant and slow. "You tell me." Her voice held an accusation, and Peter, being her twin, understood at once that she thought he'd done it himself.

Jennifer started brushing her back teeth vigorously, in case Peter was ready to confess. That way she wouldn't have to look right at him. But she saw him in the mirror shaking his head, his dark eyes furious that she'd thought—even for a moment—that he might have been the one playing the trick.

■ ■ ■

Twenty minutes later Jennifer lay in her bed— a Scottish double, which meant it was slightly larger than a single but not nearly as wide as an American double bed—and listened to Molly's soft breathing across the room. *How wonderful to be a four-year-old,* she thought, *and not have to worry about anything. Like card games that finish themselves and woods that are too big for their surroundings and locked garden cottages. To be four years old and have all mysteries solved with a healthy helping of pudding.*

Jennifer felt miserable. She was worried about Peter being changed by Scotland partly because she knew that she herself was already different. She had a secret that she'd kept for the entire day, and she'd never kept a secret from Peter before.

When you're a twin, a secret is something you *share*.

Under her pillow was the little metal key that she'd found in a beaded purse that went with the black dress in the first trunk. A tiny tag affixed to the key with a ratty piece of string read SUMMER HOOSE. She hadn't told Peter about the key, and she hadn't told him about the woods and the little white cottage, either, which she suspected was that very "Summer Hoose." She turned over and buried her head in her pillow and thought she would cry. She was *that* miserable with her secret.

Instead she fell instantly to sleep.

■ ■ ■

In the morning, though Jennifer thought she had gotten up really early—the clock said 7:00—Mom and Pop were already dressed and downstairs watching the news on television with Gran and Da.

When Jennifer walked into the room, they were all whey-faced and staring at the set. The room positively resonated with pain.

"What's wrong?" Jennifer asked, fearing a major

war or an airplane crash or whatever else it was that made grown-ups unhappy.

"Gordon McIlreavy's cornfields are full of crop circles," said Da. "A line of seven of them showed up overnight."

"Lucky the child didn't find an eraser," Gran said, "or the whole of the countryside might have gone missing. That blasted Michael Scot."

Seven

Circles

J ennifer sat down between her parents and tried to make sense of the news. It seemed that a local farmer had gone to check on his growing corn—wheat, she reminded herself—and there, to his surprise, on the south part of his field had been seven large, awkward circles all in a row, mashing down his crop.

A helicopter had taken a bird's-eye view of the fields and it flashed onto the TV screen. The crop circles looked exactly like Molly's drawings on the map.

The TV announcer discussed with an English parapsychologist the many suggestions brought forth for the origin of crop circles, including thought waves, alien invasions, and hoaxes. Neither of them mentioned a wizard's map.

"But that can't be," Jennifer said as Gran drew

the map from her apron pocket and smoothed it out on the coffee table.

They hunched over it, checking back with the television to match up the two patterns.

"It can't be," Peter, in his pajamas, echoed from the doorway.

But it was.

Even the line radiating from the last circle— where Jennifer had grabbed up the map from Molly, causing her pen to slip off the page—was indelibly etched in the corn.

They all looked at one another, stunned, except for Gran, who stared down at the map, her lips pursed thoughtfully.

"What's for breakfast?" Molly squeezed in past Peter, totally oblivious to the terror that had struck in the TV room. "I'm hungry."

Gran refolded the map carefully and shoved it back down into the deep safety of her pocket. "Porridge," she said, standing up and going into the kitchen.

"What's that?" asked Molly.

"Oatmeal," Mom answered. "Best thing for all of us."

Pop laughed, but it was a hollow sound. "The Scottish cure-all," he said.

Nobody laughed with him. Instead they marched like zombies into the kitchen after Gran.

There was an awful silence while Gran served up the porridge, accompanied by great mugs of dark tea for the grown-ups and glasses of milk for the children.

Jennifer didn't so much eat her porridge as stir it around and around with her spoon. The porridge was clumpy and the cream sat on top, refusing to be dissolved.

Across the table, Peter did the same.

Only Molly ate with any gusto, and when she'd finished, she announced, "I'm going up to the *actic* now."

"No!" they all chorused, not even bothering to correct her pronunciation.

"We're going for a walk into town," Mom said. "To the castle."

"But I want to bring the baby to the castle," Molly whined.

"She means the doll baby she found," Peter explained.

"They don't allow babies in the castle," Jennifer said quickly. As an excuse, it sounded pretty feeble, but it seemed to satisfy Molly.

"I will stay here," said Gran. "And make preparations."

No one asked her what the preparations were for.

■ ■ ■

In fact they squeezed into the rental car and drove into town by way of McIlreavy's farm, which was really the long way around. The main road quickly thinned down to a one-lane bit of blacktop lined with great hedgerows growing so thick and high, they could not see what was on the other side.

Then suddenly the hedgerows gave way to high stone walls, and the high stone walls to low ones topped by barbed wire. And beyond the wire Jennifer could see waving wheat.

From the ground it was difficult to discern any patterns at all, much less the familiar circles that had been so clear from the helicopter's view.

"How will we know where the crop circles are?" Jennifer asked, but she knew at once when, up ahead, she saw that the lane was crowded with parked cars.

Pop pulled up as close to the wall as possible, and Da hopped out, going over to the policeman who was directing traffic on the narrow road. They chatted for what seemed like forever before Da came back, his face a conflict of misery and relief.

No one in the car had said a word all that time. Not even Molly.

Da climbed back in and slammed the door.

"The police think it's boys have done the circles. They've found bootprints."

"Ah," Mom said. "But you don't look totally convinced."

"Hoofprints, too," Da said dismally.

"Michael Scot," Peter whispered to Jennifer so quietly she had to read his lips, "had a devil of a horse."

Jennifer started to shake as if she had a fever, till Molly, sitting next to her, cried out.

"Jen is hitting me, Jen is hitting me!"

Jennifer hadn't been hitting her at all; but, as she shook, her trembling arms had pushed against Molly, who was perched in the car seat.

"Let's get to that castle!" Mom said in an over-bright voice that betrayed that she was more disturbed than she dared to say. "It's going to be a fine castle day."

■ ■ ■

In fact it was not a good castle day at all. It was a bank holiday, and the castle was closed until noon. So Pop parked the car in a lot, and they walked around the town for a bit while Da explained some of its history in a distracted voice.

The town had had, Jennifer thought, an awful lot of martyrs in it. She didn't say that out loud, but Peter did.

"Blood and burnings," he whispered to her. "Burnings and blood. What a place."

Molly tired quickly of all that history, but by then it was eleven o'clock and time, according to Da, for "elevenses," which meant tea and biscuits.

"Milk and cookies," Mom explained.

So instead of waiting for the castle to open, they all agreed to go home. Pop drove rather more carefully than he had in the rain, and they arrived at Abbot's Close soon enough and safe. Tumbling from the car, Mom managed to distract Molly into the garden, but Jennifer, Peter, and their father followed Da right into the kitchen.

Gran was where they had left her at the table, the map clutched in her right hand. She was not moving but staring ahead, as if in some sort of a sitting-up coma. On the kitchen table in front of her was the Patience game, but not in any of the patterns Jennifer and Peter had played.

Across the table from Gran sat a black-eyed man with a shock of black hair that fell across his forehead like a bandage. Jennifer thought at once that he had to be an actor in a play because he was so incredibly handsome, with high cheekbones and a hawk nose. He was wearing actor's clothing, too: an odd cloak that looked at first as if it were black but shimmered strangely where the kitchen light hit it, a little like sunlight on a dark pond; a black velvet doublet; green hose; and the oddest shoes. Jennifer thought the entire outfit must be incredibly uncomfortable, but the man looked entirely at ease.

"And where's your de'il of a horse?" asked Da.

"Wherever the de'il puts him," said Michael Scot. "Yer mistress has been waiting for the lot of ye to come home. And with much patience." He smiled. It was a slow, slippery smile, without any warmth to it.

"Gran!" Molly came running in suddenly from the garden, bursting through the kitchen door and passing right in front of the stranger as if she didn't see him. Mom was right behind her.

"Can I go to the actic now?" Molly called out.

Michael Scot stood. "Ah, the one whose hand on the map called me forth. A hundred years is a long, cold wait." He stood and reached over, putting his own hand on top of Molly's glossy curls, saying, "I shall tak ye to the *actic* myself, child." With the other hand he drew his cloak around Molly, obscuring her.

There was a sudden great shaking, as if the ground were heaving itself in a troubling quake, then an immense swirl of wind. And in an instant, they were both gone.

EIGHT

Trade

For a long moment nobody moved, and then Mom screamed, an awful sound that seemed to split the air, propelling them all into action.

Da scattered the cards in front of Gran with a single sweep of his hand. The minute the pattern was broken, Gran shook herself thoroughly, like a dog coming out of a bath. Meanwhile Pop had flung his arms around Mom and she'd stopped screaming.

In the middle of this whirlwind of action, Jennifer and Peter traded oblique looks, but not a single word.

When everything had quieted down at last, Gran spoke. "I suppose you need to ken what this is all about."

"I need," Pop said in the low, slow voice that Jennifer knew meant trouble, "to know where my daughter is. And fast."

"Alas—that I dinna ken," said Gran, shaking her head. "Except that she is with Michael Scot."

"Who is seven hundred years old!" Peter's voice held all the scorn a thirteen-year-old could muster. "This is pure bull." He stalked out of the room, but then stood at the door because—Jennifer knew—he couldn't bear not to hear the rest.

"What does he want with her?" Mom asked the question Jennifer didn't dare to voice. "With Molly?"

"What do wizards ever want?" said Da. "Power and more power. And a long life to wield it."

"But Molly can't give him that," Mom wailed.

From the doorway Peter moaned. "Blood," he said.

... *and burnings.* Jennifer remembered the rest and shuddered.

"He wants the map," said Gran. "There is much of his power invested in it."

"Then why didn't he just take it?" Mom said. "Why did he have to take my little girl?"

"For a trade," said Da.

"You canna just take an object of power," Gran explained.

"It must be given." Jennifer said the words before she knew that she knew them.

Da nodded. "And I said she has the magic, Gwenfhar."

"Aye. But can she wield it?" Gran asked.

Jennifer gasped. "I don't have—" but Mom's scream cut right across whatever else she was going to say.

"Just give him the map!" Mom hadn't meant to scream the words, but they came out that way all the same. "Just give him the damned map." She began to sob silently.

Gran shook her head. "We dinna dare. The last time he had the map, from my own father, there was war and famine and—"

"There's *always* war and famine," said Peter from the door. "And always will be. Magic has nothing to do with it."

Jennifer was surprised at the withering despair in Peter's voice. He'd never spoken like that before. She had thought, as his twin, that she knew all his moods. But not this one.

"Och, laddie," said Da, "there's more to this than you ken."

"I know my little sister's been snatched up by

some...some maniac, and all he really wants is this map." In four big steps Peter was back in the room and had snatched up the map from the table. "While you all sit gabbling on about magic, I mean to give it to him."

"You canna," Da said.

"You will na," Gran said.

"Yes, I *will*," Peter cried and, turning, was in the living room and heading toward the stairs.

"Where's he going?" Pop cried desperately.

"To the attic," Jennifer said. She'd known before he started where he was going, and knew, too, that she had to go with him.

"He's going into trouble," said Gran. "Best have the cards," she called after Jennifer. "They've some meaning I dinna understand, but have them anyway."

And Jennifer, not understanding why she took the time to come back into the kitchen, picked up the two decks of Patience cards, and then ran out of the room.

■ ■ ■

As she went up the stairs two at a time, Jennifer expected her mother and father, and even Gran and Da, to follow. She expected them to phone the police or to get a gun or at the very least to offer her something for... What was the word Gran had used the day before?

Protection.

But as she went, she heard Gran cry out to the others, "Leave them. They have the twinning, which Michael Scot does not know, for they do not have the look of doubles. It will serve them well."

Even if she had not heard Gran, Jennifer would already have known with perfect clarity that no one was going to help them. Peter and she were on their own in this.

But then she realized something even more important. Gran had said an object of power could not be taken. But Peter *had* taken it from the table.

So it must have been given.

To them.

By Gran.

Which meant Gran expected them to do what the grown-ups could not.

Clutching the Patience cards to her chest, Jennifer cried out in a voice that was hopeful and terrified in equal measure, "Wait for me, Peter! Wait for me!"

NINE

Back in the Attic

Touched by a slant of light from the attic window, Peter was kneeling by one of the open trunks, weeping.

Jennifer was stunned. She couldn't remember the last time she had seen him cry. Maybe when they'd been in third grade and he'd broken his arm playing soccer. Though even then he hadn't cried in front of his teammates, but only when the doctor had begun to set the arm in plaster.

She waited before speaking, thinking he wouldn't want to know she was watching him. But it was too late. He already knew she was there.

Twins always knew.

He turned and saw her but kept on crying, his face all scrunched up and his sobs coming out in great horrible gulps.

Jennifer went over and put her hand on his back.

His sobs slowed, then stopped. When he looked up, his eyes were cloudy with tears and his voice cracked as he spoke. "Sorry, Jen. It's just... I feel so helpless. And stupid. Why did I come racing to the attic, anyway? Molly's not up here. How could she be?"

Jennifer looked around at the jumble of objects in the room. "No, she's not here now, Peter. But you were right to come. She was here just minutes ago."

Peter took a deep breath, and when he spoke again his voice was almost normal. "How can you know that?"

"Look around, Peter. What's missing?" Jennifer said, gesturing broadly with her left hand.

Peter glanced briefly. "How should I know..." Then he stopped. "The baby doll in the christening dress. The one Molly wanted to bring downstairs. It's not here."

Jennifer nodded.

"But that's impossible. It's *all* impossible."

"What it is," Jennifer said carefully, "is magic."

"But..."

And then she knew. Knew—and had to say. "You have to believe, Peter. You *have* to. Otherwise we're never going to get Molly back."

Peter stared at her in an odd way, his head to one side. He looked like some kind of bird. "How do you know that, Jen?"

"I just do." She shrugged and wished she could tell him. But there was nothing to tell. All she had was a short, sudden shock of recognition: *Here in Scotland magic is real.* Briefly she wondered if she was as crazy as Gran. Then shook her head. They were not crazy, neither one of them. "I just do," she repeated.

"But *I* don't know that," he said slowly, meaning that he was her twin and should feel the same things.

"You have to trust me on this, Peter," Jennifer said.

He hesitated before speaking. "I do." His mouth said the words but his eyes gave a more cautious answer.

"Please, Peter."

After a long moment he shrugged. "All right, Jen. I don't have much of a choice, do I?"

"No," she said. "Nor do I."

"So what's next?"

"Let's look at the map carefully," Jennifer said. "I mean *really* carefully. If Michael Scot wants it so much, we need to find out why. Gran said that much of his power is invested in it."

"What does that mean?" Peter asked. *"Invested."*

"Like a magical bank account, I think."

Still on his knees, Peter spread the map out on the table where Molly had been drawing just the day before. The map was clearly of Fairburn. Not only was the town's name under Michael Scot's, but they could identify the town features as well: High Street, where they had walked in the morning, Double Dykes Road, the castle, and the places of martyrs. There was a golden star on Abbot's Close, right where Gran and Da's cottage was situated.

"Look at these," Peter said, pointing to four pictures, one in each corner of the map. Jennifer had been so focused on the map itself, she hadn't paid them any attention.

In the upper right-hand corner was an Arab in a flowing burnoose, in the upper left a little cat sitting in a box. The bottom left picture showed four young women dressed in wedding gowns and bridal veils, carrying roses. And in the lower right-hand corner was a hideous imp with long fangs like a saber-toothed tiger's, and a strange hat on its head.

"This all reminds me of something. I can't think what it is," Jennifer said. She closed her eyes, trying to remember, then opened them again. "It's hopeless, Peter. My mind's a blank."

"Mine isn't. I know what it is—it's the games, Jen!" Peter picked up the Patience booklet. "Remember? The Sultan—well, that's the Arab. And the third game is called Puss in the Corner." He tapped the picture of the cat on the map. "And the fifth game is The Demon." His hand hovered over but did not touch the imp. "Remember how I wanted to try that one because of the name, but it was too tough to start with."

Jennifer took the Patience booklet from him and opened it to the first page. She scanned down the contents. "The game after Puss in the Corner is The Four Marriages. That must be the four women in the veils. You're a genius, Peter!"

"But, Jen—it's just riddles and a map and a game of cards," said Peter miserably. "What does it really mean? And how will it help us get Molly back?"

They stared at one another, and suddenly Jennifer went cold. She almost said a bad word under her breath. Here they were talking about playing games, and somewhere else there was a frightened little girl, just four years old, who had been stolen away. That was not a game at all.

"Oh, Peter," she said, her own voice cracking. "It's all we have."

This time it was his turn to do the comforting and hers to cry.

Ten

The Sultan

Jennifer wiped her dripping nose on her sleeve. "Sorry," she said. "I didn't mean to go *splah* on you." She didn't mention that he'd been crying earlier, because it wouldn't have helped to bring it up. He didn't mention it, either.

"We should go downstairs and tell them Molly's not here," Peter said.

"They'll have guessed by now."

It was such a sensible answer, Peter just nodded. "But where is she?" Peter said. "I mean, Michael Scot touched her and then they just...disappeared."

"Magic." Jennifer said the word with more confidence than she felt. "And the only way to get her back is with the same."

"Don't be a nitwit. We don't have any magic."

"We have the map," Jennifer said. "And the

cards. They are part of riddles. The Minor Arcana. I'm sure of it."

He looked at her oddly.

"You promised to trust me."

"Then we have to think this out carefully. Figure out what each item means." Peter looked down at the map.

"Carefully and quickly," Jennifer added unnecessarily.

Peter counted on his fingers. "The map. The cards. The turban. Maybe the doll. What else?"

Jennifer nodded at each item. "Oh no!"

"Oh no, what?"

"I forgot. I have this key." She pulled the key from her pocket and gave it to him.

He looked at the tag. "What's a summer hoose?"

"I think it means summer house. You know— a garden house. Not to live in, but to read in or to play in." Quickly Jennifer told him how she had gone into the back garden while he'd been trying out the croquet set, and how she'd gotten lost in the strange forest.

" . . . which was much bigger than it should have been." She tried explaining what she hadn't understood herself, making a complete mess of it.

Peter looked dubious.

But the moment she mentioned following the white cat, they both looked at the upper left-hand corner of the map. The puss in the box wasn't white. It wasn't any color at all.

"Still," Jennifer said, "that's one more corner that seems to have some connection with this... thing."

"I think," Peter said, "that's not quite right. I mean, I think this has more to do with the Patience games than the map."

"Patience!" Jennifer said. "That's it!"

"That's what?"

"Mother said in the car on our way here that we needed patience."

"She meant something else, Jen."

"Maybe."

He nodded. "OK—maybe."

"And we have patience now. Or rather, we have the game."

"Actually," said Peter, "it's not just one game, but a whole lot of them."

"OK—a whole lot of Patiences. And they seem to relate somehow to the map. And Michael Scot wants the map and will trade us Molly for it. So."

"So. . ."

"I think we need to *play* the games. Like Gran was doing downstairs."

"Jen—Molly is missing. We have to do more than just play cards." The crack in his voice had returned.

"Mom and Pop and Gran and Da are downstairs doing the ordinary things," Jennifer said patiently. "Like calling the police and searching the house and the garden. We can't help Molly that way. But we are twins—which Gran thinks is out of the ordinary. So what we've got to do is not the ordinary, but the extraordinary."

"Like playing Patience?"

She nodded. "We did The Star first, right?"

"And it was easy."

"Look." She pointed to the star on the map. "I think that's new. It's brighter than the rest. I don't think it was on the map until yesterday, after we played the game."

"You can't prove that, Jen."

"You can't *not* prove it," Jennifer said.

"So what does it all *mean*?"

"I don't know. I only know we have to play the games. And in the right order."

"You can't be serious."

Jennifer looked at him without flinching. "Deadly serious."

"You want to play The Sultan next?"

"Yes."

"This is crazy, Jen."

She handed him the cards. "Crazy or not, it's the right thing to do. Somehow it's the key." She put her hand over her heart. "I know it here. You shuffle and deal. I'll read out the rules."

He took the packs of cards from her. "Please, Jen, let's go downstairs."

" 'Using a single pack ...' " she began.

"I know. I know. I started The Sultan before, remember?" He took out the four kings and the ace of hearts, and set them as shown in the diagram. Then, as if he'd suddenly turned into an expert, he shuffled the rest of the pack with a magician's flair.

"You cut them," he said, handing the cards to Jennifer.

She cut the cards and handed them back, and then Peter began the game.

While Peter played, Jennifer looked once more at the map. She was sure the Arab in the right-hand corner of the paper had been wearing only a big flowing robe before. But now—as she watched—he was slowly crowned with a turban as big as his head. The turban appeared as if sketched in by an invisible pen.

"Peter," Jen said, turning to him, "look!"

"Shut up," he said, "I'm almost done. There. See—the Sultan is surrounded by his wives." He pointed to the King of Hearts, which was in the middle of the four queens. "What do you think?"

But Jennifer was no longer looking at the game. Or at the map. Instead she was staring at the play turban. It had fallen from the trunk and was lying on its side. In the middle of the turban shone a deep red stone.

ELEVEN

Patience

"Peter," Jennifer said, "that red jewel wasn't here before." She set down the booklet and went to pick up the map.

"Wasn't where?"

"In the turban. It was only a plain turban before. And it wasn't even on the map. See?"

"What *are* you talking about?" Peter asked. His voice seemed lined with resentment. He hardly even sounded like Peter.

"I don't know," Jennifer said, but softly, so as not to annoy him any more. "The map, the Patience games, the objects in the attic—they're all linked somehow. Like tumblers in a lock. Each one opens it a bit more."

"You're not making sense, Jennifer," Peter said gruffly.

"Just play the next game, Peter."

He got ready to deal out Puss in the Corner, with the kind of ferocity he usually reserved for games like soccer, shuffling the cards with quick, angry movements.

Jennifer picked up the booklet again and found the right page. " 'This game is a derivative from the original Patience,' " she read aloud, stumbling a bit over the words.

"Whatever," muttered Peter. "Hurry up, Jennifer."

" 'The first step,' " she read, " 'is to take out the four aces, and to place them face upward, so as to form a square. Having dutifully shuffled the rest of the cards...' " She continued reading till the end of the instructions, but then instead of watching Peter's cards, she glanced over at the map.

As the game progressed, card upon card, the cat in the box on the map had taken on color. It went from no color at all to a perfect pearly white, as if the invisible hand now wielded a paintbrush.

"There!" said Peter after about ten minutes. "Done."

And done, too, was the white cat on the map, its whiskers a steely grey—like wires—its eyes a shade of amber, and its nails a shimmery sort of black.

"Peter..." Jennifer began, "the map..."

But he paid no attention to her. "The Four Marriages next," he said. "Come on, Jennifer. Come on. Read to me how to set out the next tableau."

This game took both packs of cards, and Jennifer began reading even before Peter had finished shuffling the packs together.

" 'Take the first thirteen cards that come to hand.' " She stopped. "Thirteen, Peter. I'm not sure that's a good number to be playing with."

"Don't be daft," he said to her, his voice as grey and steely as the cat's whiskers. "Just read."

Wondering what "daft" was, Jennifer read.

Peter played.

And on the map, the four brides' faces were slowly drawn in with almost photographic realism.

Jennifer was startled when she realized that she actually recognized all four of the brides. One was Gran with her shiny white hair, one was Mom with that pair of deep dimples, one was Molly under glossy chestnut curls, and one was Jennifer herself, her red hair teasing from beneath a bridal veil. The white gowns suddenly shimmered like painted silk and, diagonally across the map, the white cat shimmered as well. Jennifer squinted her eyes and it seemed to her as if there were lines drawn across the map from the white of the cat to the white of the gowns.

"Peter!" she cried, grabbing as many of the cards as she could from the table. "That's enough! We're going about this the wrong way!"

He looked up at her, his eyes not Peter's eyes at all. "Gi'e me the cards, Jennifer."

His voice wasn't Peter's, either, and she realized in that moment whose voice it was. She'd only heard it speak four sentences. But the slow, drawling, commanding tone was unmistakable.

"Michael Scot!" she said, almost in a whisper.

"Too bad ye didn't let Peter play the next game," said Michael Scot. "My demon would ha'e loved him. Lads are so succulent afore they grow beards, and my imp has e'er had a monstrous sweet tooth." He laughed, a strange and awful sound, especially coming out of Peter's mouth.

"So you were the one who finished Peter's game before," she said.

"Not finished. I canna finish it. Not on my ain. Not wi'oot the map in my possession. Silly of me. But I canna resist a trick."

"What do you want from us?" Jennifer asked.

"Answer me yer own riddle, and I'll give ye the round," Michael Scot's voice in Peter's mouth replied.

Jennifer went very still. *Riddles.* One of the Minor magics. If Gran was right, then whatever Jennifer said next was terribly important. Yet how could she possibly know what the right answer was? This wasn't some silly riddle, like "Why did the chicken cross the road?" This was real. And the consequences were real.

Jennifer tried to breathe slowly and think. *What does Michael Scot want?* He had taken Molly. He needed the map. He couldn't play the card game without Peter's hands. Were any of those the answer she was looking for?

And then suddenly she remembered what Da had said—about what wizards *always* wanted.

"Power!" she answered. "And time enough to wield it."

"Och, wee lass," said the voice, "I will gi'e ye this round. Ye ha'e worked hard enough to earn it. And I did say I would." He laughed again. "This round. But nae—I think—the next!"

Then all at once, like a balloon that had lost all its air, Peter's mouth went slack, his eyes went blank, and he tumbled from his kneeling position to the attic floor.

Twelve

Into the Woods

Oh, Peter!" Jennifer cried, putting her arms around him and helping him sit up.

"Sorry, Jen, I didn't mean to blub like that. It's just...it's just I feel so helpless." He looked at her with a strange, stunned expression.

"So you said. Before."

"Before what?" He was clearly puzzled.

"Before you played the games."

"What games?"

Only then did Jennifer realize that for Peter the last half hour—the three games of Patience, the changes in the map, and all their conversations in the attic—had not occurred. When Michael Scot had taken over Peter's body and mind, Peter hadn't felt a thing. Nor did he now remember any of it. It was like the time he'd fallen from the top of the slide at the town swimming pool onto the concrete and gotten an awful concussion. Everything that happened right before—and right after—the accident was gone. Forever.

Patiently, she explained what had happened.

"Jen, this sounds crazy. *You* sound crazy."

"Any crazier," she asked, "than stealing Molly away from the kitchen while we watched?"

Peter shook his head miserably. *That* he remembered. "So what can we do?"

"Do?" She had no answer.

"Maybe we should take the map, the cards, the turban, and the key and go downstairs and find Gran and Da. After all, they seem to know more about this...crazy stuff than we do."

She searched his face for any traces of the wizard, in case he was trying to manipulate her, but the eyes were Peter's. The voice, too.

"You're right," she said.

■ ■ ■

They raced down the stairs and into the kitchen, but no one was there. No one was in the family room or the dining room or anywhere else in the house, either.

"But they wouldn't have just disappeared without leaving us a note," said Jennifer.

"Unless..." Peter said, "unless they were disappeared by force."

"Or by—magic."

Magic.

The word hung in the air between them. For a moment it silenced them both.

"Then what should we do now?" Peter asked at last.

"Call the police."

"Right—and say that a thirteenth-century wizard just stole our little sister and our parents and our sort-of grandparents in the hopes of making a trade for a map that makes crop circles when it's not being a magic bank. And that same wizard made me play three games of Patience and he has a demon that likes to have beardless boys for... for pudding? They'll put us *both* in a Scottish loony bin."

She had to admit that he was right. "Then..." She paused. "Then it's up to us to find them by ourselves."

"How?"

They were back to that again. And they might

have gone around and around, trying to figure out a logical next step and getting nowhere, but a strange sound outside the kitchen door suddenly broke through their argument.

Peter peered out the window. "Jen—there's a white cat out there, rolling around in the grass and making funny noises. Look."

Jennifer crowded next to him and looked. There indeed was the white cat, on its back, wriggling about in the raised herb garden.

"Catnip," she said to Peter.

"Catnip?"

"Gran told me she'd planted it. I thought it odd at the time."

They stared for a moment at one another, then nodded. Without needing to say a word, they knew where it was they had to go.

The minute they opened the door, the cat leaped up and ran off, toward the rose arbor.

"Come on," Jennifer said. She had the map in one hand, the key in the other. Peter was carrying the turban and the cards.

They followed the white cat through the arbor and around the great holm oak whose trunk was bound by the ironwork seat. Their feet thunked solidly on the paving stones and then crunched onto the gravel path, where the high stone wall suddenly hid Gran and Da's cottage from view.

The white cat never looked around to see if they were following, but skittered down the pathway in front of them.

Peter, who was slightly ahead of Jennifer, called over his shoulder, "How can there be this much forest in a garden?"

At the sound of his voice, the little white cat suddenly took off, straight into the woods, between two enormous, brooding trees.

Peter stopped, waiting for Jennifer to catch up with him, which she did within five steps. But instead of stopping, she passed right by him and plunged after the white cat through the dark trees.

Reluctantly, Peter had to follow.

ThIRTeeN

The Summer hoose

As soon as they got into the woods, day became dark. There were only occasional shafts of light filtering down from infrequent breaks in the green canopy above. They had to blunder along, pushing through interlacings that were filled with things that scratched and stung their hands or slapped at their faces, for the forest was trackless.

Once Jennifer thought she saw a small green snake with jeweled scales cross in front of her. Another time a dragonfly the size of a hair clip hovered on faceted wings by her face.

Peter kept seeing the liquid shine of unblinking eyes, some round as quarters, some slotted like splinters of steel, staring out at him from the brush.

They were both afraid, but still they kept on,

even more afraid to stop now that they had started. They worried about Molly and what the wizard would do with her; they worried about the disappearance of the grown-ups. But they did not worry about themselves. They felt they were somehow armored against the magic, for hadn't Jennifer already defeated the wizard once?

So they continued following the white cat, which—whenever they fell behind even the slightest bit—would stop and lick its fur until they caught up again.

"Where...are...we?" Peter said after about ten minutes of difficult slogging through the underbrush. He was breathing heavily between each word.

"In...the...woods," Jennifer answered, not bothering to either stop or turn around. She had as little breath as Peter.

"I know that!" His voice followed after her, full of exasperation; and he added, all in one big rush, "We must be going around in circles, Jen. There can't be this much forest in a walled garden."

She was about to turn on him and say something just as exasperated back, when they stumbled into the little glade. It was shimmering in full sunshine, and motes of light danced about like insects. Or fairies.

In the center of the glade was the little summer hoose. The white cat, curled in a corner of the front step, was once again fast asleep.

"Oh, Jen!" Peter said. "You were right. About the garden and the house."

She bit back a sharp reply and held up the key. "Do you want to open the door and go in first, or should I?"

■ ■ ■

All their combined courage, suddenly and without warning, seemed to leak away.

Jennifer fumbled with the key and couldn't seem to get it into the keyhole. Peter leaned halfway over, hands on knees, as if trying to catch his breath. And when the key finally fit the hole and was turned, the door creaked open—with that awful squeaking sound that signals horrors to come in a movie.

Neither one of them moved forward.

"I'll go..." Jennifer said, but didn't.

"No, I'll..." Peter started, then stopped.

The white cat stood, stretched slowly, and

arched its back. Then it brushed past Jennifer's legs, its tail tickling against her right calf, and stalked into the summer hoose, leaving them both behind.

Peter looked at Jennifer and she looked back. They shrugged away any lingering fears and followed the white cat into the little house.

Molly was sitting on a canopy bed that occupied the center of the room, looking dazed in a white bridal dress and veil. Beside her were Gran and Mom, and they were dressed the same. In Molly's lap was the doll, which now had hair as red as Jennifer's, peeking out beneath a veil.

And slumped in wicker cages hanging from the cottage ceiling were Da and Pop.

Jennifer and Peter gasped and ran to the bed, but before they could speak, the fire in the massive stone fireplace roared to life and the door slammed shut behind them.

"I thought," came Michael Scot's slow drawl, "that ye two minikins would ne'er get here...in time."

Peter turned around at once. "Let them go!" he shouted. "We'll give you what you want—just let them go."

But Jennifer did not turn. Instead she shoved the map down into her jeans pocket and whispered to her little sister, "Everything will be all right, Molls. You'll see."

Molly didn't say a word, which was unlike her, and Jennifer guessed that some magic was keeping her mouth shut. But though she couldn't speak, Molly blinked twice and a single tear fell from her right eye.

"We've got the map," Peter was saying, "if you'll trade."

Michael Scot smiled like a snake, all lips and no teeth. "Then gi'e it me."

Peter turned to Jennifer and held out his hand. "Jen?"

"No," Jennifer said. "I don't think so. Because once he's got the map, he's got us as well."

Michael Scot's smile slowly disappeared. "It doesna pay to think too long, lass. Time is all on my side."

"Time, maybe," said Jennifer, "but not right."

Michael Scot threw his head back and laughed quite heartily at that. The fire crackled as well.

"There is no right but power maks it so," he said. Then he made a strange pass with his hand

and everything—fire, cat, bed, wicker cages, sum-mer hoose, and all—disappeared.

Jennifer found herself standing on the gravel path by the great holm oak with the ironwork seat.

Alone.

FOURTEEN

Cold Iron

I will not cry, Jennifer thought. *Michael Scot is nothing more than a school bully.* She'd learned all about bullies in sixth grade, when Horace Lanoose used to taunt Peter and her about being twins. As long as Peter knuckled under to Horace, and as long as she cried, he'd kept on: two weeks of name calling and pushing and shoving. But once Peter fought back and she refused to weep anymore, Horace had left them alone. True, he looked for the smaller fifth graders, easier to bully. But she and Peter taught what they'd learned so painfully to the younger kids, and after a while, Horace had no one left to bully at all.

"I will not cry," she said aloud, and sat down on the iron bench.

"Nor sob, neither," came a voice from somewhere nearby, a rumbly sort of a voice.

"Nor blirt," came another, this one higher pitched.

"She shall not weep, nor shall she cry,
Lest sunburst blind her reddened eye," came a third, very feminine voice that had a kind of strange steel core.

"Who's there?" Jennifer whispered hoarsely, for she couldn't see anyone around.

"Who's here, you mean," said the rumbly voice.

"Who's snagging," said the high voice.

"We three as one the band do make;
The pleasure and the pain we'll take," said the womanly voice.

"Show me who you are!" cried Jennifer. Only the cracking of her own voice betrayed her fear.

"Show us your magic first, child, and then we will show you ours," said the rumbly voice.

"I..." Jennifer began. "I have no magic. I'm an American."

The three voices chuckled together.

"You would not hear us at all, had you no magic," grumbled the first voice.

"Or need," said the high voice.

"Where need is great, what spans the gap,
Love, fortune, power in..."

"The map!" whispered Jennifer hoarsely.

"The map!" agreed all three voices.

"Show it," added the grumbly voice.

"I will not give it to you," Jennifer said, more loudly than she meant to. "You cannot take it from me without my permission." She hoped Gran was right about that.

"We do not want to take it," said the rumbly voice.

"Just look at it, ye doited lass," said the high voice.

"Is this a trick?" Jennifer asked.

"A cantrip? Nae," said the high voice again. "Show us the bloody thing and be done wi' it."

The voices were argumentative and a bit silly, but she heard no real threat in them. She took a deep breath. *And what more could happen to me than has already happened?* So thinking, she reached into her pocket, drew out the map, and placed it on the iron seat next to her, smoothing it open with her hand. To her surprise, it was no longer the map of Fairburn. Gone were the streets with the odd names, gone were Molly's circles, gone was the ruined castle. Below Michael Scot's name now was a map of Gran's garden, each herb and flower bed carefully drawn in. And in the center of the woods was a dark blotch where the summer hoose should have been. A black spot over-inked, as if someone had angrily tried to blot it out.

"Well!" said the rumbly voice. "I surely hadn't expected to set eyes on that again! Himself must be in a swivet for sure."

Jennifer felt a hot breath on her hand and looked up. There above her was a great black dragon, the color of the painted iron, standing on the gravel path. His neck was crooked like the top part of a question mark as he read the map over her shoulder. By his side was a long, slim dog, like a greyhound, only long haired and totally black. Next to the dog was a black unicorn, her horn a twist of ebony.

"Who are you?" Jennifer asked. "What are you?"

"*Bound in cold iron, and not set free,*
Till maid and master in one shall be," said the unicorn, and with a quick little turn on her hind legs, she did a strange prancing dance.

"Oh," Jennifer said, suddenly remembering the three twisted legs on the iron seat—shaped like a dragon, a dog, and a unicorn. She glanced down and saw that those iron legs were now straight and blank.

"So you must be that maid and that master, though it seems unlikely," said the dragon. His neck was still crooked, but now, instead of looking at the map, he was staring into Jennifer's eyes.

The unremitting black-eyed stare made Jennifer horribly uncomfortable, as if the dragon were sizing her up for dinner. She looked away.

"This is a coil, a tangle, a very fank," said the dog, sniffing. "She wears pants. Perhaps that makes her a master, though she be no master of mine."

"I don't like dogs much, either," Jennifer replied. "I prefer cats." The dog managed to look appalled and offended at the same time. "But everyone—boys and girls—wears pants these days. Or jeans."

"Jeans?" The dog tried that word in his mouth, as if it were a new kind of bone. "Jeans. Janes. Joans. She's a jute, she is."

"Don't mind him," said the dragon. "He's Scots to the core and cannot forget it. Doesn't like much else."

"Well," Jennifer said, getting a little peeved with the three of them, but especially the dog, "if men can wear skirts here in Scotland, why can't girls wear pants?"

"Skirts? I'll skirt ye, lassie," growled the dog. "Those be kilts, nae skirts." He showed his teeth.

Remembering Horace the bully, Jennifer showed her teeth right back at the dog, and he quieted at once, looking up at her with a new kind of respect.

"Maid and master," the unicorn reminded them. *"Two as one,*
Else this magic be not done."

"Oh," said Jennifer, "I get it now."

The animals looked at her blankly.

"You see—I'm a twin."

The dog growled again and shook his head. "More coils and conundrums. How can one be a twin?"

"No, I mean I am part of a set of twins."

"Maid and master," repeated the unicorn.

"My twin is a boy," Jennifer said.

The dog gave a short, sharp laugh, an uncomfortable sound, as if he was not used to laughing.

"Himself will nae be pleased at that. Oh no. Twins be nae easily unpossessed."

"But it explains everything," the dragon said in his rumbly way.

"Nae at all, nae at all," whined the dog. "My poor head. My poor dowp." He lay down on the ground and looked miserable.

"It explains," the dragon said patiently to the dog, "why we are still the very color and feel of iron, though free of it. We must find the boy as well, I fear, before we can go from this bounden place as we once were." Turning his great head to the sky, he remarked, "What time is it, child? Neither night nor day, by the looks of it."

"Actually afternoon, I think," said Jennifer. "Or it should be." She looked up at the grey sky, which indeed gave no hint of time.

"In the world of magic there be all time and no time," said the dog. "Michael Scot maks it so."

"Time was and is and will be more,
Ere we walk free out of this door," the unicorn added mysteriously.

"Does she always do that?" asked Jennifer.

"Do what?" rumbled the dragon.

"Talk in rhyme."

The dragon smiled, which showed an enormous number of teeth. "All unicorns rhyme. It's in the blood." A small breath of smoke escaped between two of his bottom teeth.

"Ne'er mind the time. That boy—be he sprack or toustie—we need him," the dog said, standing. "Will ye tak us to him?"

That was when Jennifer finally burst into those long-held-back tears.

FIFTEEN
■ ■ ■ ■ ■ ■ ■

The Dark Trio

There, there," said the dragon to Jennifer. He was trying to be comforting, but that grumble of a voice allowed for little comfort. "There, there."

Jennifer kept on crying.

"I hate it when humans do that!" exclaimed the dog, lying down again. He put his paws over his ears. "Greetin' and carrying on. Canna ye stop her?"

"A tale can melt the hardest heart,
And make the softest feel the part," sang the unicorn.

"The only tale I have," the dragon said, "is about being bound by the iron. And to tell it would only remind the child of what she does not want to hear."

Jennifer shoved the map into her pocket and wiped away the tears with the back of her hand.

"No—tell me," she said, then snuffled. "I won't cry anymore. But tell me everything. Then maybe I'll know what to do. There's only me now, you see, to rescue them all from the wizard. Peter and Molly. And Mom and Pop. And Gran and Da." The list was so long, it ended up being a kind of plaintive wail that caused the dog to put his paws even tighter over his ears.

"Ah, child," said the dragon, "none of us knows what to do about that. We could not even rescue ourselves without your help. But if past is prologue, then you shall have it." He sat on his great black haunches, closed his eyes, and threw his head back. "I was born on a fine morning in—"

"Not *that* far past," growled the dog, taking his paws off his ears and sitting up. "Or the wizard will have her family dead and buried before we get to yer first teeth."

"I was born with all my teeth," said the dragon.

"Och—gae on with yer tronie, then, for all I care," growled the dog. "I was only trying to help, mind."

"I will get to the meat of the matter, then," said the dragon. "I was a red dragon, the color of flame. Born at the beginning of this world's turning."

"History always makes its start
Inside the storyteller's heart," the unicorn said in an aside to Jennifer.

"Please, Dragon," Jennifer said. "The dog is right. Get to the important part. Quickly. I haven't all that much time."

The black dog wriggled his rear with the compliment, his long, slim tail beating against the ground.

"IwasareddragonthecoloroflameandMichael Scotboundmeincoldiron," said the dragon, in an offended tone.

"Not quite that quickly," said Jennifer, unable to keep the exasperation out of her own voice.

"I'll tell it plain. We were all bounden by the wizard," said the dog, standing and walking slowly to where Jennifer sat. He put his long muzzle in her lap. His liquid eyes stared up at her, as if memorizing her face. "I for disobedience, the unicorn for treachery, and the dragon"—he picked his head up and stared over at the dragon—"and the dragon for being bloody boring."

"Arrrrrrrrrgh!" the dragon said, which was both a sound and a flame, black and hot. The flame licked at the dog's ears and he scooted around the back of the oak to hide there.

"Don't," said Jennifer, standing and shaking her finger at the dragon. "Don't be a bully. I can't stand bullies."

"It will take more than a finger shake to best Michael Scot," said the dragon.

"And more than a blaze of fire," replied Jennifer, "or you'd have done it before."

"He *did* do it before," said the dog, sidling out from behind the tree to stand next to Jennifer. "And that's why he was bounden. He's nae got an ounce of control. If the fire had seared the wizard instead of the wall, we had all been the better for it."

"Fire and water and wild," sang the unicorn,
"And the pearly heart of a child."

"I suppose," Jennifer said, turning to the unicorn, "that you mean the fire is the dragon and"—she guessed—"you are the water?"

"A unicorn's horn maks all water pure," explained the dog.

Without thinking, Jennifer's hand went down to the dog's head and rested there. "Then you are the wild?" she asked.

"Only when I am wi'out a master," said the dog, pushing his head up against her hand.

"And that makes me the child." Jennifer nodded. "I'm not so sure about that pearly heart, though."

"Just unicorn-talk for an innocent, a pure one," the dog said. "Don't tak a bit of notice. It's just blether. Nonsense."

"So what comes next?" Jennifer turned her gaze from one animal to the next.

"What way is next the map shall show,

As underground we all must go." The unicorn pranced on her little hooves and spun around.

"Underground? You mean like in caves?" Jennifer shuddered. "I hate that sort of thing."

"You *must* go," explained the dragon, "because a hero always goes underground in his journey." He looked at Jennifer. "Or *her* journey."

"Who says?" Jennifer asked.

"Everyone knows," said the dragon.

"Every *dragon* knows," the dog amended. "Because it's in caves that every dragon meets a hero."

Jennifer refrained from reminding them what usually happened to the dragon in such a scenario. She didn't think that blurting that out would be at all polite. Or safe. "Are you sure?" she asked the unicorn. "I mean, about the underground part."

The unicorn did not speak but, slowly and with great resolve, nodded her black head up and down three times, the ebony horn making a graceful ellipse with each pass.

Jennifer thought for a minute. She wasn't sure she trusted them completely. They were an annoying, quarrelsome trio. But if they hated Michael Scot for binding them, then they *had* to be on her side. She started to nod her agreement back, then suddenly remembered something.

"Treachery," she said slowly, "and disobedience."

"Dinna forget," the dog said, "lack of control." He bared his teeth at the dragon.

"Not much in the way of a hero's companions." Jennifer was beginning to change her mind.

"Do you have any other choice?" asked the dragon, who for once was refusing to be baited by the dog.

It is, thought Jennifer, *a question with no good answer.* "Come on, then," she said.

As if her permission was all they'd been waiting for, the dark trio surrounded her and, a bit warily, herded her back toward the spot in the forest where the summer hoose used to stand.

Sixteen

Underground

The going was easier this time because the dragon went ahead, with the unicorn right behind, and together they cut a huge swath through the underbrush. Jennifer stepped where they had stepped, in the dragon's enormous footprints and the smaller hoofprints made by the unicorn. On either side of the trail the two large creatures left a hash of broken vines, trampled flowers, and mangled plants.

"Dinna fash yerself. Dinna worry," the dog told Jennifer over and over. "Dinna be distressed." After a while, it became a whining litany.

Finally she turned on him. "How can I not be distressed, you silly mutt?"

He bowed his head but continued walking, mumbling, "I be silly. I be indeed. A silly, stupid dog. I be, however, nae a mutt. Whate'er a mutt may be."

Jennifer was immediately contrite. "Don't listen to me, Dog. I am just a bit—"

"Afraid? 'Tis all right to be afraid. I have ne'er known a hero who was not a bit afraid. A bit is all right. A lot is not."

Jennifer didn't tell him that she had gone past "a bit" back when Molly had first been taken from the house, and past "a lot" when the rest of the family had disappeared. She didn't tell him she wasn't a hero. "I just don't like caves."

Up ahead the dragon suddenly stopped and raised his great head, the long neck bending and straightening as he looked around. Beside him the unicorn stopped as well, then spun about three times on her hind legs before settling back down on all fours.

"Are we almost there?" asked Jennifer.

"Patience," cautioned the dog. He sounded so much like Mom, Jennifer's eyes got teary.

Instead of answering her question, the dragon stepped aside and Jennifer could see that his great bulk had been hiding the entrance to a cave—an entrance that was blocked by a massive wooden door.

"Well," Jennifer said in an overly bright voice.

"A locked door. Too tight to crawl through, too big to break down."

"There's a keyhole," said the dog sensibly.

"My key only opens the summer hoose door," said Jennifer.

"This *be* the summer hoose," said the dog, "in a different guise. Canna ye smell it?" He sniffed the air. "I can."

Jennifer remembered the black splotch on the map where the summer hoose should have been. Black for dark. Black for evil. Black for Michael Scot's heart.

"One door for summer, one door for fall,

One door makes winter of them all," sang the unicorn.

"There are only two doors," Jennifer pointed out.

The dragon smiled his toothy smile. "Poetic license."

Slowly Jennifer drew the key out of her pocket and put it in the keyhole. Unsurprisingly, it fit. Slowly she turned the key. There was a shallow clanking sound and then the great door swung open, revealing a long stone passageway. Jennifer pulled the key out and hesitated.

"I'll go first," said the dragon, "being that caves and dragons belong together. Even before caves and heroes."

Jennifer didn't argue, but she followed close behind. The dragon's bulky legs offered some protection, though she wasn't sure from what.

The passageway was unlit, and it wound down and down and down into the bowels of the earth. Walking behind the dragon's swinging tail, Jennifer could feel the pressure of all that stone and dirt upon her; she felt buried alive. Reaching out a hand to the wall, she recoiled at the damp and slimy feel. She began to sniffle, and she would have begun screaming as well, had the dog not come up by her side and leaned against her.

She put her right hand on his head, and as if he were a guide dog, he led her through the black tunnel of stone.

They seemed to walk forever in the dark. They'd left summer outside, with its flowers and soft breezes, and now were going where it was forever damp and cold, *Into a kind of winter,* Jennifer thought, *with this passage between being the autumn of their trip. In some ways the unicorn had been right after all. Poetic license, indeed.*

■ ■ ■

After a few more turns, Jennifer guessed that there had to be some sort of light source ahead, because now she could see a thin grey outline around the dragon's bulk, like the corona of an eclipse.

Light, she thought, breathing shallowly. *Light will help.*

The dragon moved forward several steps more, hesitated a moment, then walked through an enormous archway.

Suddenly they were in a large cavern of light, where torches—the real kind, with flames—illuminated hundreds of hanging stalactites and uprising stalagmites. In the torch glow, it looked as if the cavern had a wall of ice glittering cruelly on one side, and a wall of flickering green flame on the other. Only the far end of the cavern was still an inky black, as if a backdrop to the rest.

In the very middle of the cavern rose a stone platform as high and as wide as a bed. On it lay Molly, Gran, and Mom, with the rosy-haired doll beside them. They were all on their backs, eyes closed, looking as if they were asleep.

Or dead.

Jennifer drew in a gasping breath and then felt again the steadying pressure of the dog by her side. Slowly she walked up to the platform and saw the gentle rise and fall of breath in each body, and was comforted by that. A little.

So she left the bedside and walked around the rest of the cave, looking for some sign of Peter and Pop and Da. There—beneath great columns of the ice, she thought she could distinguish the shadows of what might have been bodies, but in the wavering light she could not be sure.

"Third time welcome," came the hateful drawling voice of Michael Scot from the dark end of the cave. "In the attic, in the hoose, and now here, in my cave. Where I have been bound up too long waiting a hand on the map."

"I do not feel very welcome," Jennifer replied, trying to spot the wizard in that vast blackness, and failing.

Under her hand the dog began to tremble, and this time it was Jennifer who did the steadying, her fingers tangled in his long black hair.

"Oh, ye are welcome, indeed, if ye ha'e brought me my map," said Michael Scot. "For it protected ye in the summer hoose but brought ye sure-footed to me in my cave."

Suddenly a shadow amid the shadows moved out into the light. Michael Scot stood next to the raised platform. Black hair, dark cape, high cheekbones, hawk nose. He was still incredibly handsome, and he smiled that snake smile, which—in the tremulous light of the cave—was even more frightening than before.

"I brought the map," said Jennifer, taking several steps backward, and stopping only because she had bumped up against the bulk of the dragon. "Or maybe it brought me. But you shall not have it."

"Oh, I shall ha'e it, lassie, I shall ha'e it very soon. And there is naught ye can do to stop me."

"My three friends shall stop you," she said, but her own voice betrayed her doubt.

Michael Scot put his head back and laughed. "These three treacherous, cowerin' beasties? I am surprised ye could unbind them at all—but they'll be as little use to ye as they were to me." He held up his right hand and counted off on his fingers. "One—a dragon so filled wi' anger he canna direct his flame. Two—a one-horn so treacherous, she canna be trusted to speak the truth. And three—that misbegotten dog that now trembles at yer side. Could ye count on such a coward? I could not. Och, lass—ye would ha'e done better on yer own."

Secretly Jennifer agreed with him. But she would not let that show. The animals had already come this far with her, showing themselves beholden for their unbinding. Besides, they were all that she had. So she said, much more boldly than she felt, "Perhaps they are . . ." and then stopped. She wasn't sure what word she wanted. Suddenly she saw a reflection of herself and the creatures in the wall of ice and knew what to say. "Perhaps they are *mirrors* of their master."

The dog made a noise, a low, throaty sound, not exactly a growl. It took a moment for Jennifer to realize he was chuckling.

"Enough of this blether," the wizard said petulantly. He snapped his fingers, and another shadow stepped out of the darkness to stand by his side. "Redcap, for yer hunger, tak the dragon."

The figure now in the light was something out of a nightmare: a muscular man-creature with skinny fingers that ended in eagle talons, large fiery red eyes that glowed in the dark, and grisly grey hair that lay lank upon his shoulders. He wore iron boots laced up with wire, a stained leather loincloth, and an odd red cap that perched on top of his head. A pikestaff was gripped tightly in his left hand.

"Ye'll like this, lass," the wizard said, once more smiling. "He delights in keeping his cap red by dipping it in blood."

"The demon," she whispered to herself, remembering that Michael Scot had said he liked to eat boys. "The last figure in a corner of the map."

As if he had heard her, Redcap grinned. His teeth were long and pointed, like a tiger's. He lifted the pikestaff and looked toward her—but he seemed to be looking through her to the dragon, who stood behind Jennifer, trembling.

Seventeen

Wizard's Power

Tak him!" ordered Michael Scot.

At his master's voice, Redcap leaped forward and, with the staff, swept Jennifer to one side. She tumbled head over heels and crashed against one of the ice columns, shattering it.

Out stumbled Peter, who, white and cold, collapsed at her feet. The turban, which had been in his possession, fell to the cave floor, spilling out the red jewel.

Jennifer was about to put her arms around him, to warm and comfort him, when an awful scream made her look up.

Redcap had stuck his pike, the cruel knife part of it, up under the dragon's chin and with a mighty shove had torn an enormous hole in the creature's throat. Then he had casually taken off his red cap and dipped it in the waterfall of blood.

The dragon was still screaming, a horrible bubbling sound, and in his agony he let go a great gout of flame that crossed the cave and seared the columns of ice. At the same time, the unicorn was stamping its hooves on the cave floor, making a rat-tat-a-tatting like a funeral drum.

"No!" Jennifer cried, and started forward to help, even knowing she could not get there in time. So she picked up the jewel, which was now as large as a baseball, thinking maybe she could throw it at the demon and distract him.

But the minute she put her hand on the jewel, the hideous Redcap screamed and dropped the pikestaff, though no one had touched him.

Jennifer looked down at the jewel in her hand. It was pulsing like a heart. She squeezed it, and Redcap screamed again.

Quite determinedly, she took the key and scratched it along the surface of the jewel. The key left a deep mark in the red stone, and it looked like a wound welling up with blood. When she looked back at Redcap, down the right side of his forehead and across his bulging red eye was a thin line, like a nail scratch. The eye was weeping red tears. She knew the dragon, in its dying, had never touched him.

Magic, she thought, and remembered the

strange lines that seemed to connect the white cat diagonally across the map with the white brides. She squinted down at the red jewel and saw similar lines stretching across the cave to the monster's hat.

"Redcap!" she cried, and when he looked over at her with his one good eye, she put the jewel on the cave floor and—quite without anger—stomped down with all her strength on the red jewel, shattering it into a dozen pieces.

Redcap screamed again, and—as if he had been made of clay—he shattered as well.

For a moment there was silence in the cave. Then Michael Scot spoke in his drawling voice.

"One for one," he said. "I'd call that a draw. But monsters are so easy to come by. I dinna think ye have enough friends to spare."

It was his casual dismissal of the two creatures that undid Jennifer. Ignoring the wizard's implied threat, she went over and knelt by the side of the dying dragon. Lifting his massive head in her hands, she looked into the dark eyes that were slowly shuttering.

"Now you are truly free," she whispered, a catch in her voice.

The dragon gave a great convulsion; trembling waves ran down his length, to the very tip of his tail. Then he lay still, a black unmoving shadow beneath her hands.

Standing, Jennifer faced the wizard. "What guarantees will you give me for the map?" she asked.

"Your family intact," he said.

"And free?"

He smiled. It was an odd sort of smile. "What is freedom, after all?" he asked. "Are ye not noo a slave—to yer parents, to yer country, to yer king?"

"Americans have no king," said Jennifer. "We fought a war about that."

Michael Scot, though, was not listening to her as he warmed to his topic. "A slave to fashion, a slave to desires, a slave to passions. How can ye think yersel' free?"

While he was speaking, Jennifer saw—out of the corner of her eye—that Peter was slowly standing up. And the ice columns that had been melted by the dragon's dying flame had uncovered Pop and Da, who—having shaken themselves warm—had quietly sneaked over to the closest side of the stone bed, where Gran and Mom lay close together.

"...a slave to the calendar, a slave to duty, a slave to deadlines," Michael Scot was saying.

Pop and Da slipped the still-sleeping women off the stone bed, as they were the nearest, and were going back for Molly before the wizard noticed them.

Turning, he raised a hand. "Touch that lass and I shall do mair than merely kill ye."

"The map," Jennifer whispered hoarsely, not trusting her voice any more than that. She took it from her pocket, unfolded it, and dropped it on the floor.

Behind her Peter gasped. But Jennifer, after a quick glance down at the map, knew what she had to do. "I will give it to you," she said, "for the promise of my family's and friends' freedom."

"Do ye," came that slow, malevolent voice again, "trust me, lass?"

"Not for a minute," Jennifer whispered. Then she shoved the parchment toward him with her foot.

He bent down to pick it up, and Peter scuttled behind him, ran to the stone bed, grabbed up Molly, and, clutching her limp body, raced down one of the twisting tunnels.

The wizard seemed not to notice. Instead he screamed in agony. "What is this? What cantrip is this?" He stood, holding the map aloft.

No longer the map of Scotland or Fairburn, or the garden map that Jennifer had spread out on the iron seat. Now it was the map of a single, deeply buried cavern.

Gran's voice floated across the stones toward him, weak but plain. "Ye were once a generous man, Michael Scot, wi' a heart as large and as full as Scotland itself, so the map ye invested yer soul in then was as large. But when ye turned to the black arts, yer soul shrank till it became the size and color of a lump of coal. Ye have drawn and redrawn the borders of yer heart, Michael Scot. All yer magic is noo confined to this pinprick of a place."

"Then ye shall be confined wi' me, old woman! Ye and the rest of yer cursed clan!" the wizard screamed as he crushed the map in his hand. He pointed his other hand at the unicorn. "De'il, I free ye!"

Some thin stream of old power shot across in flame at the black creature, who began to glow. The ebony horn sheered off but never landed; or if it did so, it landed soundlessly. The unicorn seemed to stretch and grow under the fire spell. Bigger at the shoulder, longer at the leg, higher at the haunch, greater at the head. And when it was done, instead of the dainty black prancer who had accompanied Jennifer into the cave, there stood a stunning ebony stallion, eyes wild, with a black mane standing about its glorious head like the rays of a falling star.

"Michael Scot," said Da in a low voice, "had a devil of a horse."

And a traitor of a horse, Jennifer thought, realizing that the last time the unicorn had spoken had been at the door of the cave.

"Find that boy and his little sister, and bring them back here to me," cried Michael Scot.

For a long calculating moment the horse was still, and Michael Scot raised his hand. "Do ye mean to betray me again? Did ye like that prancing form so much, ye wish to own it for evermore?"

The dog, who'd been silent all the while, howled in his misery, then leaped for the wizard's throat. But a casual wave of that powerful hand and the dog dropped, trembling at his feet.

Jennifer gasped. What chance had they now?

"I will get to ye in the end," Michael Scot warned the cowering dog.

The black horse—mind obviously made up—galloped down the path after Peter and Molly, hooves drawing sparks from the stone floor.

Michael Scot laughed. "I will get to *all* of ye in the end."

EIGHTEEN

Fire and Ice

The wizard threw the crumpled map on the cave floor and angrily turned to Gran.

"Old woman, weak are yer powers. I shall ha'e ye slave for me fore'er, be these cave walls the borders of my kingdom."

Gran, at least, did not shrink from him. "My powers alone, perhaps, are weak, Michael Scot. But do not underestimate the powers of the children."

"They are Americans," the wizard said, laughing again. "And admit to none."

Jennifer's thoughts remained bleak. Michael Scot was right. They had no powers to compete with his. They were all weak, not just Gran. They were weak and lost.

But Gran didn't stop arguing, and while she argued, Michael Scot kept a watchful eye on

Gran—and on the other grown-ups as well. Even Jennifer was in his sight as he spoke. But he'd neglected to watch the cowering dog, who had begun to hunch away from him.

At first Jennifer was disgusted with the dog's cowardly, servile behavior. But as he slowly moved, crabwise, away from the wizard, she saw that there was method in his movements. He was scuttling ever closer and closer to the discarded map.

She knew he could not take the thing up. It might have been thrown down by the wizard, but—as Gran had warned before—a magic thing could not simply be taken. It had to be given. So Michael Scot had flung it down without any fear that someone else could get it.

Obviously the dog knew this, too, for he did not try to pick up the map in his mouth. Instead, on his belly before the parchment—as if he were sniffing at the thing—he breathed.

Not in—but out.

That small breath—that tiny movement—powered the crumpled map, and it began to slide along the cave floor, pushed by the wind from the dog's nose. In the smallest of increments, the map moved away from the wizard and toward the wall of green fire, the crouching dog behind.

Startled, Jennifer realized what the dog was attempting. *Surely,* she thought, *I can distract the wizard long enough for the dog to succeed. Maybe we can win against Michael Scot without using any magic at all.* She began walking toward the wizard so as to draw his attention to her, and so his back was firmly set to the creeping dog.

"Leave my Gran alone," Jennifer called, shaking her finger at the wizard. "Or I'll—"

"Or ye'll what?" Michael Scot asked. His voice was fully confident and had lost that drawling quality that—Jennifer suddenly understood—had been just for show. The wizard hadn't been entirely sure of his ability to win, not sure at all. And that knowledge made Jennifer secretly pleased.

She was trying to think of a response to Michael Scot's question, something to disturb his new confidence, when she heard the sound of the devil's hooves returning down the corridor back to the cave.

Oh, Peter, she thought miserably. *Oh, Molly.* Her mood suddenly swung back toward bleakness and despair.

She turned to look at the horse and was as surprised as Michael Scot, for the horse had returned to the cave without the two children.

"Did ye nae bring them back?" the wizard cried.

The horse bowed its great neck. "Gone, my lord."

"Dead, ye mean?"

The horse did not answer but kept its head bowed.

Behind the stone bed, Mom screamed once and was still, though Pop cursed and kept on cursing for a full minute, using words Jennifer had never heard before, but whose meanings she knew at once.

"Ye appalling libbit, ye great gomeril!" Michael Scot cried. "I needed that bairn for my spells." He was practically foaming at the mouth in his fury. "With her pearly heart I might ha'e managed to enlarge the map. But not noo. Not noo!"

Jennifer turned her head away, biting her lip so she wouldn't cry. She couldn't really believe it. Molly dead? And Peter? *Peter.* They were twins, as close as close. Surely she would have felt something if he were gone. But, just as surely, the horse wouldn't lie to his master.

Then she saw that the dog was still at his slow

task, inching closer and closer to the wall of fire with each courageous breath, blowing the map in which the wizard's power was invested. She knew she had to put aside her own agony and sorrow, and help.

"Michael Scot!" she called, turning back to him. "Beware. If my brother is dead, my other half, then I have all the powers myself." She remembered a bit from the movie they'd seen on the plane coming over to Scotland. The hero had marched right up to the bad guy, and while he walked, all eyes were on him. No one saw what else was going on behind.

So she walked close to the wizard, within a hand's breadth of him, waggling her finger right up under his nose.

The dog's soft breath pushed the paper toward the wall of fire.

And Pop, having exhausted his store of curses, took that moment to leap on the stone bed, and then launch himself onto the wizard's back.

"Avaunt!" Michael Scot cried, raising his hand toward the hurtling man.

"Avaunt yourself!" cried Jennifer, lifting her own hand—without knowing any spells at all, but wishing, and making Mr. Spock's Vulcan sign. She struck the wizard's hand with her own, and she could feel a surge of awful power, like a lightning strike, run down his arm and into her fingers.

There was a sudden roar of flames rushing from the fire wall, and suddenly Michael Scot was afire, his black hair burning, his black cloak burning, his dark doublet burning, his green hose shimmering with flames.

Jennifer stepped back from the excruciating heat and turned her face away.

Pop fell to the floor, hands beating frantically at his own clothes, which were on fire as well. Gran and Da raced around the stone bed to roll him on the floor till the flames went out. At the same time, Mom raced to Jennifer and held her in a tight embrace.

No one thought to help Michael Scot, who continued to burn with a fierce green flame until he was only a pile of grey ash.

The horse waited until the wizard was truly gone, then whinnied once, loudly.

Safe in her mother's warm embrace, Jennifer heard footsteps coming down one of the long corridors.

"Mom," Peter called, "Pop! We're safe. We're safe." He came into the cave from the corridor, dragging Molly behind. "The horse told us to wait till he called."

Mom opened her arms and scooped Molly up. Da put his hand on Peter's shoulder. Gran helped Pop to stand.

Only Jennifer, still wondering if she'd actually defeated the wizard on her own, heard the whimper by the wall. Turning, she saw that the dog was now as grey as stone, his nose badly seared by the flames. He lay on his side breathing shallowly, quickly, as if he'd just come in from a long run. She went over to him and knelt down.

"*You* are the real hero," she whispered. "You— not me."

The dog pushed his head up against her hand.

Nineteen

Ashes

Carefully Gran swept up Michael Scot's ashes into a white handkerchief that Da had had in his pocket. Then, with Peter and Da supporting Pop, with the dog set upon the horse's back and steadied by Jennifer's constant hand, and with Molly comfortably between Mom and Gran, they traveled back through the long stone passage into the light.

It was still afternoon, the sun slanting down through breaks in the forest canopy.

Jennifer turned once to look again at the cave entrance, but the cave had disappeared. The little white summer hoose was there in its stead, the white cat fast asleep on the steps. Jennifer tried squinting and thought she could see—as if through a shimmering curtain—the outline of a darker, bigger, rounder entrance imposed over the house's small door. But then a bit of sun slashed down and broke that vision into dancing motes of light.

■ ■ ■

After Pop had been to the doctor and gotten some cream—"unguent," Da had called it—for his burns, and after the vet had seen to the dog's nose, they bought a takeout order of fish and chips and all sat in the garden, around the wrought-iron table, and ate a casual dinner. No one spoke about what had happened in the cave. In fact, for a long time no one spoke at all.

The horse stood in the middle of the lawn, cropping contentedly at the grass. The dog lay by Jennifer's foot, but there was an alertness in his long, lean body, and though his head was down, he did not close his eyes. Both animals acted as if they belonged in Gran's garden, and—Jennifer thought—in a way they did.

Molly soon fell asleep, her head in Mom's lap. And Pop, tired from his burns, went upstairs to bed.

"I'll take the wee bairn to her room," said Da, carrying Molly off.

"I'll come, too," said Mom. "I'm exhausted. All that running around." She followed after him.

Jennifer wondered if they were remembering what had really happened, or if it would all retreat to the substance of a dream.

"Is he truly gone?" Peter asked Gran. "The wizard, I mean."

Gran pulled out the handkerchief and untied the knot. The grey ashes lay in the center of the white linen square. "What do you think?"

Peter shrugged silently.

Jennifer shivered and answered for him. "We don't know."

From the lawn, the horse cleared its throat. "Michael Scot once told me that if he died in fire, his ashes should be set out for the birds. A raven and a dove will come and circle above them. If the raven comes down to get the ashes, then the ashes should be scattered to the winds. But if the dove tries to bear them away, the ashes should be given a Christian burial."

"A *Christian* burial?" Peter was outraged. "He was too evil for that."

Gran shook her head. " 'Evil' is a strong word, Peter. Once he was a good man. But the black arts changed him. Still, at the end of the day, we dinna ken what was truly in his heart."

The dog at Jennifer's feet growled.

"Or if he even *had* a heart," Peter muttered. "Do you know what he did to the horse?"

Jennifer knew Peter was not asking a real question. He already knew the answer and was about to tell them.

"He thought the horse had betrayed him and so he punished him in the worst possible way."

"A unicorn is a *worst possible way?*" Gran smiled.

"A big, strong stallion turned into a mincing, prancing female!" said Peter passionately. "And reciting poetry!"

Gran and Jennifer broke into laughter, and then Jennifer thought—with a bit of an ache—that she and Peter had moved very far apart this vacation. And summer had only just begun.

Though it was evening, the sun was still high, as it always is in Scotland in July. The ashes in the handkerchief seemed such a small reminder of a man.

Jennifer looked around the garden, trying hard to listen for birds.

"I don't hear any," Jennifer said.

"Hearing is a gift," said Gran. "Perhaps it's nae yers. Ye have other compensations. Ye understood about Color Correspondences wi'out being told. And about the Rule of Giving. And Riddles."

But the dog suddenly sat up, his ears twitching back and forth. "They come!" he said.

Jennifer strained to hear something. Anything.

"I hear it!" said Peter.

"I don't," Jennifer complained.

"Patience is a virtue," said Gran.

"Patience is a game," Jennifer and Peter said together.

The twin thing, Jennifer thought, and smiled. Maybe they hadn't moved so very far apart after all.

Then Jennifer heard the raw croaking of a raven from a long way away. And closer in, the cooing of a dove.

The sound of wings circled overhead, and then both birds floated down closer and closer to the table where the ashes lay.

Just then a flash of white leaped onto the table-top and the cat stood, straddling the handker-chief. It swatted at the circling birds and hissed at them till they both flew off.

"So what does that mean?" asked Peter.

"It means that Gran is a greater wizard than Michael Scot," said Jennifer. "The cat is hers, after all."

Gran laughed. "I'm nae wizard at all. I thought you kenned that."

The dog sat up, looking warily at the white cat. "The cat be a dead giveaway," he said.

"Aye—that she be."

"What do you mean?" Peter asked.

It was Jennifer who understood. "Gran's not a wizard, Peter. She's a witch."

"Aye, that I be," said Gran. She wrapped the white linen back over the ashes, tied the ends in a knot, and slipped the handkerchief into her pocket. "A white witch. The best in Fife. And who better to keep an eye on Michael Scot's ashes?"

Peter looked at Jennifer and winked. "And I suppose I'm a warlock?"

"Maybe ye are, and maybe yer nae," said Gran. "It'll take practice—and patience—to find out."

"We've got the patience," said Jennifer.

"Ye surely do noo," said Gran. "Ye surely do."

A Scottish Glossary

avaunt—away

bairn—a young child

biscuits—cookies

blether—nonsense

blirt—a sudden burst of grief or anger, or to weep and sob

braw—fine, splendid

cantrip—a charm, spell, or mischievous trick

corn—wheat

canna—cannot, or can't

daft—crazy

de'il—devil

dinna—do not, or don't

doited—stupid, bewildered

dowp—hind end or bottom

dreech—a grey downpour of rain

elevenses—an 11:00 A.M. snack

fank—a noose or coil or tangle

fash—to bother, to worry, or to distress

gomeril—loud-talking fool

greeting—crying, lamenting

jute—a weak, worthless woman

ken—to know

kilt—a garment, originally worn by a Highland man, that looks like a knee-length pleated skirt

laddie—boy, young man

lass—girl, young woman

libbit—gelding

mair—more

mak—make

minikin—derisive term for a small man or woman

nae—not

noo—now

porridge—oatmeal

pudding—dessert

snagging—taunting, reproving, or scolding

sprack—alert, lively

tak—take

tea—dinner

torch—flashlight

toustie—quarrelsome, contentious

tronie—a tedious story that bores the listener who has heard it before

wee—little, very little